Greenfly

Tom Lee

Greenfly

[signature: Tom Lee]

HARVILL SECKER LONDON

Published by Harvill Secker 2009

2 4 6 8 10 9 7 5 3 1

Some of these stories have previously appeared in the following publications:
'Berlin', *The Dublin Review* (No. 26, Spring 2007)
'Cerology', *Zoetrope: All-story* (Vol. 9, No. 1, Spring 2005) and
The Dublin Review (No. 12, Autumn 2003)
'Greenfly!', *Goldfish Anthology* (ed. Sara Grant, 2006)
'The Ice Palace', *Zembla Magazine* (Issue 2, December 2003)
'San Francisco', *Draft Magazine* (Issue 1, Spring 2005)
'Island 21', *Tell Tales Anthology* (ed. Courttia Newland, 2004)

First published in Great Britain in 2009 by
HARVILL SECKER
Random House, 20 Vauxhall Bridge Road
London SW1V 2SA

www.rbooks.co.uk

Addresses for companies within
The Random House Group Limited can be found at: www.randomhouse.co.uk/offices.htm

The Random House Group Limited Reg. No. 954009

A CIP catalogue record for this book is available from the British Library

ISBN 9781846551949

The Random House Group Limited supports The Forest Stewardship
Council (FSC), the leading international forest certification organisation. All our titles that
are printed on Greenpeace approved FSC certified paper carry the FSC logo. Our paper
procurement policy can be found at www.rbooks.co.uk/environment

Mixed Sources
Product group from well-managed
forests and other controlled sources
www.fsc.org Cert no. TT-COC-2139
© 1996 Forest Stewardship Council

Typeset in Quadraat by Palimpsest Book Production Limited,
Grangemouth, Stirlingshire

Printed and bound in Great Britain by
Clays Ltd, St Ives plc

For E de Z

Contents

Berlin

CAROLINE, MY WIFE, IS FEELING UNWELL. IT SEEMS THAT THE city is not agreeing with her. We are sitting on a bench in the Lustgarten, looking across the road to the Palace of the Republic. I had hoped we would be able to go in but the building is closed, a rusting, derelict hulk deemed unsafe due to structural flaws, asbestos, or – it seems possible – more symbolic dangers.

The palace was the nerve centre of the German Democratic Republic, a paranoid state obsessed with the duplicity of its own people. It presents four walls of oily, bronzed glass intended, it seems, to conceal everything that went on inside it but which now conceal nothing, I imagine, except gutted offices, dim and draughty corridors. Instead, reflected in the glass is a corrupted, cubist vision of the city around it – shards of the cathedral's copper-green dome, Karl-Liebknecht-Strasse, the Spree River and roiling sky. Now some want it knocked down, while others would have it preserved as a reminder of the crimes committed inside.

I have been explaining this to my wife but now she is lying down on the grass with her eyes closed. Her face is flushed. She says she feels dizzy.

'It's so depressing here,' says Caroline, not opening her eyes. 'So grey, so much concrete, so many terrible things. I feel like I can't breathe.'

The city is much as I had imagined it: cold and grand,

claustrophobic with history. The architecture is monumental, designed to intimidate. In the great plazas and boulevards I find it hard not to think of grainy black-and-white film, thousands marching, crowds raked with searchlights. As we have criss-crossed the city under my direction, my wife has proved a reluctant tourist. She seems oppressed by everything – the run-down buildings near our hotel in the old East of the city, the incomprehensible graffiti that covers them, the surprising quietness of the streets. She complains frequently of tiredness. We have argued. She has decided that my interest in the city is unsavoury, voyeuristic.

'A strange thing,' I say, shutting the guidebook and sitting down next to her on the damp grass. 'Something that strikes you when you read about it is that throughout the war, even very late on when many Germans must have known it was lost, life just seemed to go on as usual. People had dinner parties. They saw friends, went to parks, bars, the theatre. They even went on holiday. Everything was heading towards this disaster, this catastrophe really. Thousands were dying all over Europe but, amid the chaos, in some ways life just went on as usual.'

Caroline does not speak. She opens her eyes briefly to check my expression. Lately she has become suspicious of everything I say. She believes that everything is innuendo, an accusation or a trap.

It is spotting with rain.

'Ready to go on?' I say.

'Please,' she says. 'I have to go back to the hotel.'

Two months ago I discovered that my wife was having an affair. She was so careless in her deceptions, so reckless in her choice of lover – a friend of ours – that I believe she wanted me to catch her, that she wished to punish me and make me suffer. There were plenty of clues, and anyway I was not so surprised.

I let the affair continue for several weeks – keeping track of her movements, imagining their meetings. In the end it played out like melodrama: the husband arriving home unexpectedly from work, the opening of the bedroom door, the wife and her lover momentarily oblivious to their discovery. Perhaps it sounds strange but this is what I had wanted to see – for her to know I had seen – so that there could be no excusing or reducing it, no pretending it was something other than this, no softening with words or regret.

I insisted on knowing everything: the wheres, hows and how oftens. I made her relive it in every detail. I put her through that; I felt I was entitled. This went on for days and eventually she told me all of it. When I revealed that I had known for some time, she raged at me, as if I were somehow responsible. There were scenes, dreadful scenes, in which everything seemed to be at an end, but in time we both relented. She was remorseful. I took some of the blame – I had been inattentive, absorbed in work.

It was then that I proposed the trip away. I remember it clearly. We were sitting in the kitchen. Soft autumn light fell in a band across the table between us. Outside in the garden the leaves on the trees were yellow gold and for a moment it seemed that it had all been nothing more than a bad dream. I had bought a guidebook and Caroline sat, turning the pages. Of course she had visions of somewhere exotic – Brazil, Mexico, the Caribbean. That was what she was used to after all.

'Germany?' she said. 'In November?'

* * *

Greenfly

I am reminded of this as we sit in the restaurant at the top of the Fernsehturm in Alexanderplatz, eating the tasteless and expensive food common to all such places. I have the lobster, Caroline the steak. We are sharing a bottle of white wine, although Caroline has barely touched her glass. Outside the clouds are turning pink in a wintry sky.

The Fernsehturm provides the best views of the city. Over Caroline's shoulder are the Soviet housing blocks and great revolutionary boulevards of East Berlin. Behind me is the vast green space of the Tiergarten, once the private hunting ground of Prussian kings. I have pointed out the landmarks we have visited in the past three days and traced the line of the now-absent Wall through the city. Now she says that she is not hungry, that her steak is overcooked, and the sight of the city far below us is making her nauseous. At the next table a young couple whisper excitedly to one another, honeymooners perhaps. On the other side, two children are jabbing at each other with their cutlery while their parents pick at their food and ignore them. One of the children begins to cry and the manager comes over and speaks quietly to their father.

'I was reading about the Stasi this afternoon,' I say. 'Apparently they used to keep samples of the body odour of anyone they thought was a criminal or a danger to the Republic. They arrested the person on some pretext and then swabbed their crotch with a cloth or broke into their apartment and stole some of their underwear. Then they kept the cloth or underwear in a glass jar. Specially trained dogs were used to recognise the presence of a particular person's odour at an illegal meeting or whatever. Smell-differentiation dogs they called them. Unpleasant, but very effective.'

My wife does not seem to have been listening. She stands

to go to the toilet and I see people at other tables turn to look at her. I am one of those men who want a woman in relation to how much other men want her. My wife is not beautiful. Her face is too angular, her expression too uncompromising for that. But she has a self-assurance, a physicality in her manner and her movements that causes men to imagine her in a particular way. I know this because I once imagined her in this way myself.

On our very first holiday together we walked through a market in Morocco. Caroline was inappropriately dressed, her arms and legs bare, and stallholders stared at her and muttered to each other. One man pushed past us and, it seemed to me, rubbed himself provocatively against Caroline's body. I turned on him and began to shout and threaten him absurdly. Other people intervened and I was pulled away. Caroline brushed the incident off – 'Men,' she said – but I could not be calmed down and insisted we return to the hotel. There she lay on the bed, baffled and amused, while I urgently and repeatedly made love to her.

'I've been sick,' says my wife when she returns to the table. She is pale, angry, a little unsteady on her feet. To her left, in the distance, are the glassy new towers of Potsdamer Platz, sign of Berlin's modern rebirth.

When I wake up in the night my wife is sitting on the edge of the bed in the hotel room, crying. This is very unlike her. I have only seen her cry two or three times before; she did not even cry when I told her I knew about her affair. She does it awkwardly, wretchedly, her body bent over itself, as if she is in physical pain. I notice that one of her legs is shaking. White light coming through the blinds – street light or moonlight, I cannot tell – lies in bars across her body.

'What's the matter?' I ask.

'Nothing,' she says. 'A bad dream. Go back to sleep.'

A bad dream. Perhaps. But I look at her and I wonder if it is something else.

I have always been a jealous man. When my wife began her affair she believed she was hurting me. She did not realise that the deepest desire of the jealous man is to have his jealousy vindicated. She believed she was acting independently, in her own interests. Now she sees that she was manipulated – I made her feel unwanted, I put temptation in her way – that I had already fantasised this role for her. She feels as if it were me who had been unfaithful, as if she were the one who had been betrayed.

Caroline's face is wet, her eyes red from crying, and as I look at her I see that thing that other men see in her. I reach out and put my hand on her shoulder. Her body tenses but she does not move away. I move my hand to her breast and begin to kiss her throat. Abruptly she stands and crosses the room to the toilet. I hear the click of the lock. The bars of light lie flat across the bed where she has been sitting.

I wanted my wife to have an affair so that I could resent her and punish her for it. I wanted to suffer and to make her suffer to prove that we were still in love. If it is a game then it is one I am winning.

On our last day in Berlin we get to the Jewish Museum around midday. I am keen to see all that we can before our flight leaves this evening and already we have visited two of the remaining sites on my list – Checkpoint Charlie and the Wall Museum. Caroline is tired and wants to stop for lunch.

'It's awful,' she says, looking up at the museum. 'So – I don't know – unnecessary.'

'Tell that to the Jews,' I say.

'I mean the architecture,' she says wearily. 'I don't feel so good. I don't think I want to go in.'

After a while she gives in, unwilling to argue, but inside she trails behind and we become separated. The museum is a labyrinth of zigzagging corridors and odd-shaped rooms, walls leaning in or out at an angle and floors that slope abruptly up or down. Dim light comes through narrow windows slashed diagonally in the walls. I wander from room to room, pausing only briefly over the exhibits – on religious life, domestic tradition, the middle class – which are somehow not what I had expected, or hoped for. After half an hour or so I realise that I am coming to the same rooms over and over again. I sense that this is deliberate, that there is some conceptual scheme at work, but the meaning of it is obscure. I find it only frustrating, claustro-phobic, and begin to look for a way out.

I arrive in a bare, high-ceilinged room without exhibits which I feel certain I have entered earlier from another direc-tion. It is immediately clear that in the few moments before I walked in some sort of disturbance has occurred. Voices are raised above the usual hush of the museum. There is some kind of disruption in the usual movement of people, a small but perceptible sense of alarm. Then I see that everyone is looking in the same direction – towards a knot of crouching people, and a woman sitting on the floor among them.

At first I do not recognise my wife. Her skirt is rucked up above her knees and her hair has escaped from its clips and hangs in tangles around her face. One of her legs is twisted under her and the other sticks out in front. Her face is red and a livid bruise is coming up around her eye, and for a moment I think she must have been attacked. Two of the museum staff are kneeling down next to her. One has his arm around her shoulders to support her and the other is holding a glass of water and fanning her face with a museum leaflet. The top two buttons of her shirt have been undone. Another man, a doctor perhaps, takes her pulse and speaks to her steadily. Altogether there is a strange intimacy to the scene. The contents of my wife's bag have spilled out onto the floor: her purse, sunglasses, phone, a packet of tissues and a small notebook. A lipstick has rolled into a far corner. Another member of staff walks around collecting them up and for some reason it is the sight of all these familiar things scattered across the room that is the most startling thing.

Other visitors to the museum, perhaps ten or fifteen of them, stand around, unwilling to move on. The atmosphere is strange, heightened, and I have the odd sensation that something profound has occurred, something that because of my late arrival I am barred from understanding. I cannot think how I should act or what I should be doing and for a moment I imagine myself to be just another passer-by, on my way through the museum, to whom the scene is a riddle, a mystery to be unravelled. What has happened to this woman? Where are her friends? She has a ring on her finger – where is her husband? I imagine myself as someone with a different afternoon ahead, a different life, to whom this will soon seem like only a minor incident in a busy day.

Someone has brought Caroline a chair and the museum staff are helping her onto it. All these people, all so solicitous

– but then it is easy to take care of strangers. I am thinking this when suddenly my wife looks up and sees me. At first I do not speak or move. Then I hurry forward.

When we finally check in at the airport, hours later, there are no adjacent seats available on the plane. I watch from two rows back as the man next to Caroline offers her his window seat and then helps put her bag in the compartment above. She is a different woman from the one sprawled on the floor of the museum. She has changed her clothes, put her hair up and applied lipstick. Only the purpling bruise around her eye, incongruous with rest of her appearance, is a reminder of the events of the day.

Once we are in the air Caroline begins to talk to the man next to her. He is smartly dressed, professional-looking, Germanic. Anyone might think they were together. Caroline's manner is light, animated, as if a weight has been lifted from her. She points out of the window, perhaps showing him some of the things she has seen on our trip. Now that the city is receding below us, she finally seems able to appreciate it. Perhaps she is reimagining it in her mind already, a list of places visited and meals eaten, a holiday like any other.

The man laughs and I wonder what she has said that is funny. Perhaps she is explaining how she came to have the bruise around her eye. Maybe she tells him the usual story: I walked into a door, I fell down the stairs. Or maybe she tells him how she fainted in the Jewish Museum, making it comic, absurd, full of melodramatic detail, a story at her own expense. I wonder if, in explanation, she tells him about our trip to the hospital, how the doctor turned to me – not to her, to me – and said, in perfect English, 'Perhaps you did not realise? Congratulations, everyone is perfectly healthy.' Perhaps the man next to her congratulates her too.

I look past the person sitting next to me and out of the window. I can see the Fernsehturm, the Reichstag and the green rectangle of the Tiergarten, and I trace the line of the Wall through the city. From the air Berlin seems innocuous, like any other city, a greying sprawl gradually giving way to fields. They say that former Stasi men still meet secretly in dingy bars to exchange information and plot surveillance. They use the old code words and signals and act as if the Wall had never come down. They cannot let go of their old habits and do not seem to notice that they are an irrelevance, that everyone else has moved on.

Half an hour into the flight Caroline stands to go the toilet, smiling and apologising. It seems to me that there is something different about her, something indefinable, a subtle confidence or a new awareness in the way she holds herself or the way she moves. I wonder if any of the other passengers who are watching her notice it, if they understand what it means, and, if they do, whether they could appreciate the terrible completeness of my victory. When Caroline passes me I reach out and touch her. Startled, she cries out. People turn in their seats. She looks down and sees me. 'It's OK,' she says, 'it's my husband,' and walks on down the aisle.

Cerology

I.

SOMETIMES, OVER DINNER, MY GREAT-GRANDFATHER, professor of anatomy at the University of O——, would describe to his wife the fruits of his most recent research. According to my great-grandmother's diaries, the Professor frequently became so absorbed in the subject which most exercised him, the structure and formation of the human brain, that he would begin to illustrate his points by arranging the food on the table in front of him. My great-grandfather would rise from his chair and, using a fork to pin down a side of lamb, a joint of pork, or a chicken, proceed to make expert incisions demonstrating the location of the cerebellum, the temporal lobe, or the medulla oblongata. A variety of vegetables, appropriately dismembered, might be added to dramatise the presence of special features, a tumour perhaps, or an evolutionary quirk. The monologues, rich in Latin terms and other archaisms, continued for a number of minutes despite – if the diaries are to be believed – my great-grandmother's vocal protestations. Once finished he would sit in silence for a few moments, sipping wine and staring thoughtfully at the transmuted items on the table in front of him, before picking up his knife and fork and returning to his dinner with renewed vigour. On one evening, 5 August 1897, when my great-grandmother had returned to her room with a violently disturbed stomach, the diaries note: 'Yet again the Professor's inability to leave his obsessions behind in the laboratory ruined a perfectly good meal. During his lecture I was tempted to describe to him in detail the results of my own extensive research into the anatomical curiosities and unusual proclivities of his faculty colleagues. I refrained only because of our daughter's presence at the dinner table and because I believe such information would do little to diminish my husband's appetite.'

The diaries came into my possession six months ago on the death of my grandmother at the age of 101. In her will she bequeathed to me, her only granddaughter, a small sum of money and the thirteen volumes bound in red leather, presumably passed on to her by her own mother and eventually found mouldering in a box in the attic of her house. Somewhat miffed that the Victorian chaise longue I had coveted ever since I had played on it as a child had gone to a distant aunt, and that I would have to be content with a merely sentimental gift, I dumped the box in a remote corner of my study. There it quickly became engulfed in books and papers, destined to be rediscovered only at some point in the distant future, perhaps upon my own death. I continued working on an essay, 'The Fantastic Vagina: Sigmund Freud and the Narratives of Edgar Allan Poe', that I was writing for an American publication.

Then, a few weeks later, in an uncanny coincidence of timing, I received a phone call from a man introducing himself as Mr H. G. Sutphen, secretary of Amicorum Cerologicorum, a society dedicated to 'the appreciation and exploration of the ideas of Professor Frederick Zoosa, your great-grandfather'. In a voice so frail, dusty and formal that it might have been calling from another century, he invited me to attend, as honorary guest, an annual lunch held to honour the Professor's work. He had tracked me down through the unusual family name and with the help of a computer-literate niece. 'Modern technology,' he said, 'wonderful thing . . .'

I was aware that my great-grandfather had been an academic of obscure interests. When I began my doctorate a number of relations, embarrassed by my field of study and desperate for something relevant to say, alluded to him as my professional predecessor. No one, however, seemed clear as to what these interests might have been, nor apparently were they very interested. Family lore had it simply that he was 'rather eccentric' – a description they no doubt now applied to me – and he was otherwise a forgotten figure.

I gently declined Sutphen's offer and, after putting down the phone, continued work on my essay. Later that evening, however, when the final corrections were complete, I discovered that my interest had been piqued. I unearthed the box, sat down and opened the first volume of the diaries.

In 1895 – about three years after the birth of his daughter Alice – my great-grandfather, a precocious young professor, published a study entitled *Cerology: Steps Towards a Science of Character*. He claimed to have come across this new field by accident while pursuing his more general research. He had, the Professor said, begun to notice certain correlations between what was known about the donors of the brains he was examining and the brains themselves. Following this intuition, he had set up a project to chart the features of over one thousand laboratory brains against detailed biographical information. In an introduction to the study, the Professor stated the basic tenets of his theory:

> The brain is the organ of the mind. The mind is composed of multiple, distinct and innate faculties which can be divided into the desirable and the undesirable, e.g., on the one hand, Benevolence, Virtue, Piety, and on the other, Mendacity, Madness, Sloth. The presence and proliferation of these faculties is represented by the brain's readily apparent physical properties – shape, size, colour, temperature, density and odour. Therefore, examination of the exposed brain allows straightforward and accurate assessment of these faculties and, when properly analysed, can be used to construct a complete and scientific portrait of the character of the deceased.

The study went on to establish a set of guidelines – 'the Index to Character', he called it – which could accurately predict anything from temperament to social class to the subject's predisposition towards criminal behaviour. Much of the second half of the study was taken up by a comprehensive list of the 'multiple, distinct and innate faculties' and their corresponding physical manifestations. For example, a brain with a dullish purple tinge, an apparent enlargement of the left lateral ventricle and a faint but detectable odour of cabbage was, the Professor alleged, conclusive evidence of a subject's proneness to bouts of melancholia and morbidity. Extensive appendices contained charts, logarithmic tables and elaborate diagrams that allowed the cross-referencing of different faculties and provided the means to arrive at a 'precise and nuanced' analysis.

Many of his colleagues at the university expressed astonishment that the well-regarded Professor had taken such an alarming turn into a field which had long been the preserve of quacks and cranks and gentleman amateurs and which, they said, was better suited to fairground tents and freak shows than to academia. In a letter to *The Anatomist*, one eminent figure even went so far as to question the Professor's mental health, quipping, 'It seems reasonable to wonder what an examination of Professor Zoosa's own brain might reveal.'

My great-grandfather, however, was unrepentant, writing in return that 'any apparent resemblance to the popular practices of Phrenology, Craniology and Physiognomy, which are no more than pseudoscience and mumbo-jumbery, is entirely erroneous. My colleagues have failed to look at the substance of the research and have instead drawn conclusions based on their own prejudices and competitive jealousies.'

All of this is a matter of public record. A visit to the university archives where my great-grandfather's papers are kept, a survey of the scientific literature of the period, a useful bibliography provided in the online journal of Amicorum Cerologicorum – it did not take much to unravel the details of the Professor's career. However, perhaps the fullest and most interesting insight to the story – what you might call an alternative history – and which until now has been unknown to all but the protagonists, comes from the diaries of my great-grandmother, Nancy Zoosa.

The diaries begin on 25 September 1891, the day after her marriage to my great-grandfather, and were written conscientiously every evening in red ink and a handwriting style weighted with baroque swirls, loops and tails. They end abruptly and without warning on 6 November 1904. From the outset Nancy's interest in her husband's work, what she called 'his brains', seems to have been minimal. When it is mentioned it is normally in a tone of mocking condescension, with the implication that men will be men and must be allowed their proud dreams of leaving a mark on the world. Instead, the greater part of the diaries concentrate on giving a full and, even by modern standards, remarkably frank account of her sexual exploits during the period of her married life.

Perhaps because she was bored, or because she was neglected by her hardworking husband – or perhaps for neither reason – Nancy began to develop an increasingly exotic appetite for carnal gratification in all its forms. In often pungent language the diaries record the details of numerous encounters – some engineered, but more often spontaneous. They include the occasional sketch to illuminate her descriptions, and a number of terms and expressions that either are of her own invention or have since fallen into disuse.

To a large extent her partners and accomplices, both men and women, were those with whom she came into contact socially via her life as an academic's wife, from an emeritus professor of antiquities ('remarkable stamina') to the Professor's own research assistant ('spirited but clumsy'). One entry, for 21 June 1895, a few weeks before the publication of the seminal paper, records the Professor's inopportune return from his laboratory to my great-grandparents' house.

Having completed a late breakfast of toast and kippers, I was enjoying the attentions of the cook when the

Professor stepped into the drawing room, apparently looking for something he had forgotten or mislaid. Although I could see my husband clearly from my reclining position on the chaise longue, the young man's eyes were focused elsewhere, and his ears were powerfully muffled, and he therefore did not pause in his – surprisingly adept – investigations. It was not shock on the Professor's face, but he stood for some moments or even minutes by the door bearing a most inscrutable expression before picking up the file he had returned for and leaving the room.

Contrary to the obscurity that many had predicted for him, in the few years following his initial study the Professor found his ideas taken up by a motley collection of maverick scientists, thinkers and political factions. If the varying agendas of his new allies – an unlikely mixture of the progressive, the reactionary and the hare-brained – troubled him, his papers do not record it. The website of Amicorum Cerologicorum provides biographies of many of these supporters, among them 'spiritualist and inventor' Godfrey Hallberg, who had become infamous for his proposal to 'construct, for the purposes of travel and commerce, a tunnel linking the south coast of England to Continental Europe'. Then, in 1899, the University of C—, arch-rival of my great-grandfather's current employer (and with a reputation as a centre for radical thought), offered to create for him a professorship in the field he himself had discovered.

Soon after my great-grandparents' arrival in C— it became clear that, by 'happy accident', the university's radical agenda was matched by an enlightened attitude towards sexual habit. 'It is most refreshing,' notes a diary entry one week after their arrival, 'to find such an intellectual openness towards fornication, even if the scholars do not always complete the transition from theory into practice successfully.' It is hard to gauge the Professor's own attitude towards this permissive environment, except what might be speculated on the basis of his later actions. The diaries omit any mention of marital conjugation, beyond a passing reference in the very first entry to 'the disappointments of my wedding night' (which, nevertheless, produced my grandmother). It is unclear whether this was because it had ceased to take place or because Nancy regarded the act occurring within the sanctity of wedlock as too banal to merit recording.

In C— the Professor was soon consumed by his work, publishing a paper that listed a number of additional faculties within the brain and their corresponding physical manifestations – all undesirable – among them: vanity venality and vulgarity. Nancy pursued her own distractions. Meanwhile, Alice, their only child, was growing into a happy, healthy girl. The diaries note that in contrast to my great-grandfather's aloofness towards his wife, he was not a distant parent. Striking a begrudging note, Nancy wrote: 'The Professor, despite his characteristic coldness and pomposity, demonstrates a surprising tenderness towards his daughter. When he plays with her and teases her, it is possible to see traces of the human feeling that is at almost all other times absent. It is clear that he is moved by her guilelessness and innocence, although of course she is growing up fast and will not be a child forever. On the whole, however, he still prefers the company of his brains to that of his family.' In the evenings the Professor returned to his study, leaving his wife and daughter to sit by the fire in the drawing room where, while my grandmother drew childish pictures and wrote in notebooks, her mother would leaf through books of drawings by Aubrey Beardsley, which she confessed to finding 'so delightful', or lose herself in the verse and novels of various French writers of the period.

2.

'I would like,' the Professor began the University of C—'s 1901 lecture for The Furtherment of the Public Understanding of Science, 'to say a little more about the physical properties of the brain and the relative implications for the behaviour and character of the individual.' The Professor pulled on some curtain cords to reveal an enlarged scientific drawing of a human brain. 'Here, for example,' he said, pointing at the image with a cane, 'is the brain of a man convicted of stealing a crate of herring and various other minor offences. We can see a flattening of the anterior horn. There is a small depression here in the substantia corticalis. On initial examination the brain also gave off a strong metallic odour. All of this is consistent with a life of petty thievery and common fraud. However,' he went on, 'it is in fact the case that in the most fundamental areas this brain differs only superficially from the brain of a normal, that is to say law-abiding and socially well-adjusted, individual.'

Then, in what according to contemporary newspaper accounts appeared to be a carefully choreographed moment, the Professor paused to put on some laboratory gloves while an assistant wheeled out a trolley upon which sat a large glass jar. Inside the jar a brain could be seen floating murkily in a viscous orange fluid. One eyewitness described how, still rocking from the movement of the trolley, the brain would emerge every few seconds to bounce gently against the glass. 'Here,' the Professor said, abruptly unstopping the jar and retrieving the brain, 'we have something quite different – the brain of a man convicted and hung for treason and other crimes of the most serious nature.' He walked to the front of the podium holding the brain aloft. Fluid dripped from it, observers noted, and ran down the lengths of my great-grandfather's gloves. He turned it around so that his audience might view its various aspects. 'Even to the unscientific eye,' my great-grandfather went on, 'radical differences from the archetypal brain are immediately evident, almost as if it belonged to a different species – an interesting debate we will not delay ourselves with here. The squared-off rather than gently curved contours, the excessively swollen frontal lobe that finds expression in the abnormally high forehead, the scaly appearance of the organ's surface, and the sharp tang of mustard that even now greets the nostrils: all these are evidence of chronic deviancy, a man, were he not already dead, entirely without hope of rehabilitation.'

The onstage drama produced murmurings of both assent and unease from the gathered audience. However, Nancy, who was sitting in the front row, does not seem to have been paying close attention. She remarked in the diaries that evening: 'The Professor's lecture went on interminably. I drew some satisfaction from observing the ranks of the cultivated and respectable, some of them well known to me. Their moustaches waxed to an absurd and improbable stiffness, their bodies contorted into poses of earnest concentration, I could not help but think of them as so many beasts dressed up to be men, their true natures scratching and inflamed underneath their heavy suits, constrictive collars and pressed shirts.' As I turned to read this entry for the first time, a folded piece of paper fluttered out. It was a copy of the programme for the lecture, on the rear of which were a series of sketches that, though crudely done, were unmistakable as representations of male genitalia. Above each sketch was the scrawled name of an individual, many of whom are known to have been present in the hall. Below the sketches was written one sentence enclosed in quotation marks: 'It is unequivocally true to say that the differing sizes and shapes have a direct relationship with the kind and degree of pleasure produced.' Whether these approximations were based on personal enquiry, or simply her undoubtedly vivid imagination, it is not possible to say.

'I am obliged at this stage,' the Professor continued, having laid the brain back on the trolley, 'to admit to a mistake in my original formulations. At that time I had concluded, somewhat hastily and in the belief that I could not have stumbled quite by accident on a discovery of such astonishing significance, that these physical properties of the brain acted as a reflection, if you like, a map, of the different human faculties. However, my research has now led me to precisely the opposite conclusion. The physical properties exist prior to, and in fact govern, the expression of these faculties.' The Professor picked the brain up from the trolley. 'I have established absolutely,' he said, 'that anti-social behaviour is caused by physical abnormality.' He paused to survey his audience. 'I need hardly say that the implications of this are dramatic.'

At this point a great fuss broke out among the audience. There was heckling. A woman vomited into her lap, and an elderly man shouted a stream of abuse before fainting in the aisle and having to be carried from the hall. Amid the fracas the Professor stood unmoved at the front of the stage, still holding the brain aloft, the orange fluid gathering in a puddle at his feet.

The Professor had become energetic in the public promotion of his work. Encouraged by his supporters, he began to extend the scope of his theories beyond the purely scientific. He was mocked by many who worked in other disciplines, but there were those, internal university documents reveal, who were alarmed at the wide sympathy his views attracted and were no longer sure whether to find him ridiculous or dangerous.

There was no thaw in relations between my great-grandparents. They ate evening meals in silence, sitting far apart at opposite ends of the dining table. The Professor took to reading books, journals and newspapers as they ate, apparently scouring them for mention of himself or his work and muttering or exclaiming at what he found. Afterwards he would retire to his study or the laboratory he had created in the basement of the house. Nancy, for her part, had begun developing ideas, in the form of sketches and descriptions in her diaries, for a range of sexual positions based on the shapes and actions of musical instruments. Having by accident – during an interval between the third and fourth movements of Berlioz's *Symphonie Fantastique* and with the assistance of the vice chancellor's wife – arrived at what she called 'the tuba', she began to experiment with models for the oboe, violin and trumpet. In an entry for 19 December 1902, she declared her intention to 'document and personally execute a position for every instrument in the orchestra – a symphony of pleasure, if you will'. While some of these positions are relatively conventional, differing only in detail from the mainstream, in other cases I am obliged to salute my ancestor's athleticism and spirit of adventure.

Of Alice at this time, the diaries note:

She is ten years old now and is developing, as has been noted with approval by others, and to my own relief, far more in the mould of her mother than in the image of the Professor. However, my husband and our daughter remain as close as ever. They have, at his suggestion, been taking long walks in the hills and forests of the local countryside. I have been able to glean little about what transpires on these walks except that the Professor speaks to her of the natural world and its scientific mysteries with the knowledge and passion that once, although it seems a lifetime ago, endeared him to me. Also, she says, he asks her questions and then listens carefully to her responses. As to the nature of these questions she will not be drawn. On their return the Professor's perennially grey and stony countenance is instead pinkish from the country air and appears softened with traces of pleasure or satisfaction. It is not long, however, before he disappears once more into the laboratory.

By 1904 the Professor claimed to have identified absolute and significant differences between the male and female brains, and the brains of different races. He had also determined, as he wrote in his notes and underlined heavily, that 'most, if not all, abnormalities are inherited'. His supporters, who liked to mention my great-grandfather's name in the same breath as Darwin or Marx, were many of them men of wealth and influence – industrialists, philanthropists, politicians, artists. Nancy, who seems to have remained entirely indifferent to the storm blowing around her husband, described a reception held in order to announce the convening of Amicorum Cerologicorum.

28 August 1904. The Professor was in his element, full of smiles and bonhomie, a sight quite as gruesome and disturbing as anything his critics might accuse him of. Our daughter, her presence requested by the Professor himself, wandered through the room carrying trays of canapés and hors d'oeuvres and attracting the complimentary words and glances of the assembled guests. They were not a promising bunch, red-faced and overfed sycophants, hanging on the Professor's every word. The evening dragged profoundly and I found myself trapped in a windowless corner between the twittering pomposities of the vice chancellor and, not for the first time, the predatory intentions of Gilbert Sutphen, the wet-lipped mayor of C—. In my boredom I fell to idly arranging a plate of food in such a way that it presented an image of edible coitus. It was almost a relief when I saw that the Professor had moved to the centre of the room and was addressing his guests. 'It is, I admit, a utopian vision,' he intoned in his new affected style. 'We are not ashamed of being utopians. Crime, political unrest, juvenile delinquency, antisocial behaviour of all kinds. We can treat these problems before they occur. There will be no need for the inexact methods or false comforts of law and order, psychiatry, or religion.' The Professor paused and beckoned to Alice, standing at the back of the room. The guests parted to let her through, their eyes ranging over her

as she walked towards her father. 'Throughout history,' the Professor said, taking her under his arm, 'individuals have been left to suffer at the hands of their abnormal behaviours and debased desires. Many would seem to prefer that it remained so. And yet we would not let a lunatic suffer in this way, or indeed a horse that was lame, or a dog afflicted with the mange. You would not deprive it of treatment to relieve its pain. It is vested interests who oppose our aims – the judges, doctors and priests whose status and authority depend on the perpetuation of unnecessary evils. Imagine, gentlemen, the society we could create. Imagine the society we could create for our children.' During the Professor's speech I had become aware of something stuck in my throat, part of the collage of food that I had previously created. I began to cough and choke, and the mayor slapped me on the back and then helped me to the door. The Professor, meanwhile, had gone back to mingling with his guests and was oblivious to my discomfort. Alice had disappeared. Still coughing fitfully I asked the mayor to accompany me into the garden. After a few minutes I began to feel somewhat recovered and there, under the boughs of the lime tree, and with the complicity of the mayor himself, I was able finally to expedite the contortions necessary for 'the bassoon', thereby completing the symphony and somewhat redeeming the evening.

Tucked inside the back cover of the thirteenth and only half-completed volume of the diaries is a photograph of my great-grandparents. On the reverse, in Nancy's handwriting, is written simply 'The Wedding'. She is sitting in the centre of the picture while the Professor stands to the right, one hand gripping the top of her chair. The pose, with its vase of flowers and table of ornaments, is stiff and formally arranged but Nancy appears relaxed. Only nineteen, dark-haired, liquid-eyed, and with the small bright red mouth I have inherited in common with all the women of the family, she looks directly into the camera with an expression of ironic amusement. My great-grandfather appears as uncomfortable as she is at ease. He seems to have been in receipt of an uncompromising haircut and, although he was nearly ten years older than his wife, his posture and features have the awkward rawness of an adolescent. He is looking away from the camera, frowning slightly, preoccupied.

There is little to remark upon in the last volume of Nancy's diaries between the evening of the symphony's completion and the diaries' sudden cessation three months later. The final entry is itself innocuous. 'A day of reading and relaxation,' Nancy wrote. 'The doctor came round by appointment in the afternoon to perform his regular examination. He commented that the Professor's daughter, who opened the door to him, is becoming a comely young girl and enquired as to whether she had begun her womanly cycle. The Professor himself has not been seen for days, as he is preparing for another public lecture to be given at the university tomorrow evening. I dare say I will be obliged to be there in body, if not in spirit.'

Despite the diaries' silence, the scenes in the university's main hall on 7 November 1904 can be easily recreated from court records: my great-grandfather's appearance on the lecture-hall stage to warm applause; the introductory remarks regarding the perfection of new surgical techniques; the screen set up to one side of the stage and eventually removed to reveal a body, that of his twelve-year-old daughter, lying heavily sedated on the operating table. The lecture, if it can be called that, never got under way. It is clear that the authorities had prior intelligence as to my great-grandfather's intentions, for as he pulled on his apron and gloves and instructed his assistant to pass him a scalpel, a dozen or so plain-clothed policemen swarmed onto the stage. The testimony of several witnesses describes how, at this point, realising that his career was about to reach a premature climax, the Professor brandished the scalpel in an unambiguous fashion and turned to meet his assailants. This last image, however, I tend to attribute to the excitability and rather Gothic imagination of these observers, for I believe my great-grandfather was not, at heart, a violent man. Indeed, there is no clear evidence of a descent into this kind of farce, nor of any blood being spilled, and I think it more likely that he allowed himself to be led peacefully from the building. Amid the drama, Alice herself seems to have been forgotten. Contemporary accounts make no further mention of her and I can only assume that she continued to lie there, drugged, on the operating table, bliss-fully unaware of her narrow escape, no more or less innocent than any sleeping child.

Months later, at his trial, the Professor's lecture notes, re-covered from the hall at the time of the raid, were quoted in evidence against him. They make uncomfortable reading. 'Until the present time we have been confined to drawing conclusions about the character of the deceased. Now, with the advances gained from research and experimentation, we can examine the living brain and, more significantly, we can operate to eradicate the cancer of abnormal behaviour.' The notes – I can hardly bear to read them – anticipate the findings of the operation that was never carried out. 'An inflamed occipital lobe, governing sexual impulse . . . the atrophied semiovale, seat of moral sensibility . . . the telltale whiff of ammonia.'

My great-grandfather did not go to prison. He insisted throughout the trial – and right up until his death – that he had been attempting to heal my grandmother of an affliction that would otherwise scar her life, and the judge accepted his lawyer's plea of diminished responsibility. He was instead confined to a Swiss sanatorium where he continued his scientific studies, publishing papers on the unusual pollination habits of a particular mountain wild flower, *Primula allionii* 'Zoosa', which to this day bears his name.

The operation that my great-grandfather intended to perform, had it gone ahead, would almost certainly have lobotomised his daughter, perhaps condemning her to the kind of imbecilic innocence that his vision seemed to favour. Alice is dead now and unable to answer questions about her childhood or the events that dramatically marked its end. Presumably she had read her mother's diaries. I can only guess at her intentions in passing them on to me.

In the melee following the Professor's arrest, Nancy's reaction – for she was undoubtedly present in the hall – goes unrecorded. Within two years, however, she had divorced the Professor and was married again, to the heir of an American railroad fortune who brought Alice up as his own child. Did Nancy continue the promiscuous habits of her first marriage? In the absence of further testimony there is no way of knowing, but I prefer to think that she did. Regardless, the diaries are her legacy. Now that my research is complete I intend to publish an illustrated edition of my great-grandmother's symphony, both for its value as a historical document and – I can vouch for this personally – the benefits of its application.

Greenfly

DURING THE TIME WHEN B AND I FIRST STARTED TELLING each other we were in love, one of the conversations we used to have was about how injured, disabled, disfigured or otherwise debilitated we would have to be to make the other fall out of love. I said we should draw up a document which specified what level of injury would release us from the obligations of being in love. B said he'd still push me around if I lost both my legs. I said I'd empty his colostomy bag if he had to have one. B said he'd feel justified leaving me if I had 90 per cent or more burns but anything else was fine. I said I didn't care if he was burnt to a crisp as long as his dick could still stand up.

I noticed the greenfly problem on a Friday night. B was watching TV, a documentary I think, and I was playing backgammon on the computer. The adverts came on and B said: 'Martin's coming over to dinner next week. He's thinking of buying a place round here. OK with you?'

'I can hardly stop him.'

'I meant about dinner.'

'I know what you meant,' I said.

'His girlfriend's coming too. She works in TV. You'll like her.' The adverts finished – the final freeze-frame seemed to last forever – and B's programme came back on. I carried on at the computer and had just brought my last counter home, winning the game narrowly, when something broke my concentration – perhaps the light flickered or there was some slight noise. I looked away from the screen and up at the ceiling. Spreading out from around the light fitting were lots of little specks, too many to count, each with their own little shadow. I stood on a chair to get a closer look.

'Janey?' said B.

'We've been invaded by greenfly,' I said.

'You're blocking the light.'

I got down from the chair and went into the kitchen. The greenfly were swarming over the ceiling there too. I went into the bathroom, the bedroom, then the spare bedroom. It was the same thing. I stood in the doorway of the living room.

'We're infested.'

'Hold on a minute, Janey. I just want to see this.'

A couple of minutes later the programme finished. B turned off the TV and stood up. He stretched and looked at his watch. He flinched when he saw me and then tried to look like he hadn't.

'I'm off to bed,' he said. 'Big day tomorrow.'

'Every day's a big day,' I said, putting on the American drawl we sometimes used.

'Sure is, baby,' said B, smiling, and speaking in the same accent. 'So that's OK about dinner?'

I nodded.

'Great,' he said. 'It'll be fun.'

B went to bed and I looked up at the ceiling. A funny time of year for insects, I thought, standing there. I shut all the windows, turned out the lights and went to bed in the spare room.

* * *

As usual, I slept badly. When I got up I looked into the bedroom, but B had already gone to work, even though it was Saturday. The greenfly were everywhere. Too little light or not enough air, either way, they were all dead. Everywhere. Greenfly on the bed, along windowsills, on the floor, on kitchen surfaces, on the top of cupboards and picture frames, the TV and the computer. There were green specks in the sugar, in plant pots, on dirty plates and bowls. Thousands of little deaths, all delicately rigid and contorted.

I began to clean up. There was something satisfying about the way they covered every surface. I wondered if they all died at the same time and fell throughout the flat, a sudden, thick green rain. Or if they dropped one by one when they ran out of light, or air, or whatever it was they needed. Did they die and then fall, or perhaps weaken, lose their grip, the unlucky ones drowning, flailing, in the toilet bowl or a half-drunk cup of coffee? The possibilities were endless. Maybe they only lived for a day anyway – some insects were like that, I knew.

It took me until about midday to clean up. After lunch I went over the surfaces with bleach, because it seemed like the right thing to do. Then I showered and washed my hair. A few little bodies spun around the plughole before darting down.

B phoned at six to say that he and 'Marty' were going for a beer and maybe some food. 'I won't be late,' he said.

After dinner I switched on the computer and played a few games of backgammon. At level five I won half and the computer won half. The technique I use is to move the counters up slowly, keeping them close together and evenly spread, until I can block out the whole final quarter. Then, with at least one of their counters out of play, my opponent is unable to take their go until I release a space. At this point I can take my time rolling, bringing up my other counters and cleaning up any of the other player's stray pieces. This strategy gives the most consistently good results and has the added advantage of attacking your opponent psychologically. Frustrated, trapped, they invariably end up doing something reckless. This was the technique I used to beat B when he and I played – when we first lived together and on holiday. 'Passive-aggressive,' he called it, and he may have been right. About a year ago B said he found the game boring. I said: 'Always losing is boring. But spare a thought for me. Always winning is boring too.'

At some point I must have fallen asleep. Normally I take a nap in the afternoon to make up for not sleeping so well at night, but I had been preoccupied with the cleaning and forgot. I woke up in the computer chair, my hand still on the mouse. The screen saver was scrolling around and around: 'All play and no work makes Janey a dull girl. All play and no work . . .' The first time B saw it he laughed, but that was months ago. The windows were black and still open and the greenfly had returned. Their shadows wavered slightly in the breeze, like tiny flames.

I swore aloud, more for effect than out of feeling. It was careless, I thought, falling asleep like that. It made me smile, though, when I thought of the girl slumbering at her computer like some fairy-tale ogre, while the greenfly rushed through the open window, attracted to the homely glow. I considered turning the lights off and leaving the window open. Perhaps they would leave of their own accord. But perhaps more would come. I didn't want to risk it. The thought of them floating down on me in the night was unsettling, and on top of that I had no wish to spend my Sunday cleaning.

I closed the windows and got the vacuum cleaner out. It was quite awkward and I felt a little ridiculous. I was glad there was no one else to see me doing it, standing on a chair, vacuuming the ceiling. I did the same in each room.

Before going to bed I wrote a note: 'Don't open windows or leave lights on. GREENFLY!'

In the morning I was pleased to see no sign of the invaders. I hadn't heard B come in, so I supposed it must have been late. He got up at lunchtime, made some toast and put on the TV. There was an old film on, the one where Kirk Douglas has his eye pecked out by an eagle.

In an advert break B said: 'Martin's invited us away for a weekend. His parents own a cottage on the coast.' Martin is one of B's workpeople. I hadn't met him but I pictured him to be quite handsome, better looking than B anyway. Since Martin joined B's firm, B can't stop talking about him. Men are just like children when they make a new friend.

'Why don't you go on your own?'

'Susannah will be there as well. It'd be odd if you didn't go.'

'Would it?'

B didn't say anything. I said: 'Did you see my note about the greenfly?' B pointed at the screen. The film had come back on and a great Viking feast was in progress. I went back to the backgammon, winning one game and losing two.

After a while the adverts came on again.

'What were you saying?' said B.

'Could you hold on?' I said. 'I just want to see this ad. I'm particularly interested in this product.'

B sighed. 'Janey, you've got to stop living your life from behind a hedge.' B's company spend a fortune sending him on courses where they teach him to say things like that.

'I think they're coming up from the canal.'

'What?' said B.

'The greenfly. They're probably attracted to stagnant water.'

'Give it a rest, Janey. I've been non-stop all week. I don't want to spend my day off talking about fucking bugs.'

'Greenfly,' I said.

I went and lay on the bed in the spare room. A few minutes later the phone rang. B answered it and I heard his voice brighten, though I couldn't hear the words. I heard him put the phone down and start whistling quietly to himself. It was a new thing, this whistling. Then he knocked on the door and came in. He stood in the doorway, fidgeting.

'I'm sorry,' he said. 'It's just . . . if you didn't have so much time on your hands, maybe you wouldn't get so . . .' He paused and looked at his palms, pretending to search for the appropriate word. I propped my head up on my hand to listen. 'So obsessive about things. Have you thought about going back to work?' He paused again. 'Sometimes it's not good to think too much.'

'Thanks for the advice,' I said. They should put that last comment on his gravestone.

'Anyway, that was Marty. We're going to shoot some pool at a bar he knows. We'll talk about things tomorrow, OK?'

I heard B come in later, but it was after midnight and I was already in bed, trying to sleep.

In the morning there were greenfly everywhere, dead again. It was as if I had never cleared up the first time and had just been ignoring their presence. But of course this was a whole other batch, a new generation in all likelihood. In the bedroom a window was open.

Using a broom and a dustpan and brush I swept the greenfly into ten little heaps. Then, out of curiosity, I gathered them all together and made a pile about as big as my fist. There must have been thousands of them. All balanced on top of each other it looked like some complicated molecular structure from a science book.

I was just about to flush the whole lot down the toilet when the phone rang. It was B.

'I've fixed up for a guy to come round and finish the tiling. Will you be in?'

'There's every possibility.'

'It'd be nice to have the apartment finished for dinner tomorrow.' B paused, perhaps waiting for me to speak. I was confused for a second when he said 'apartment' but then I realised he meant our flat. 'Any thoughts about our conversation yesterday?' he went on. I listened to the grey hum of office noise coming over the line: voices, air conditioning, electronics. 'Janey, have you –'

'What conversation?' I said.

'About going back to work.'

'I haven't had time. I've been non-stop. Clearing up all the greenfly you let in when you opened your window.'

'For Christ's sake, Janey.' B lowered his voice; I imagined people in his office looking over. 'Forget about the damn bugs. Get over it. The builder's coming at three.'

'Greenfly,' I said. But he had already hung up.

Sweeping the pile into the dustpan, I went into the bedroom, drew back the duvet and shook the greenfly out over the sheets.

The builder buzzed just after three. I looked at his face bobbing on the monitor and then let him in. I could see he was impressed by the flat. It is quite impressive, though sometimes I have to be reminded of that. It is situated in a sought-after block in a desirable location, as the estate agent put it. The building is a converted textile factory and that was one of the things B said he liked, the sense of history. We are on the fifth floor, overlooking the canal, and there is a good view across the city. It was the last flat in the block and up until we moved in it was used as the 'show home' and temporary offices of the estate agent. As a result it was expensively done out in up-to-the-minute interior decoration – reclaimed wood floors in the living room and bedrooms, slate floors in the hall and kitchen, designer kitchen units, bathroom suite and furniture. When we bought the flat they threw in all these interiors at a knock-down price. Of course they had little bits of damage: floors marked by all the shoes that had traipsed through, greasy stains from where endless anonymous hands had fingered things, but nothing you'd notice if you weren't actively looking for it. Nevertheless, it was a stretch for us – and if my salary is stopped then I don't know what we'll do – but once B saw it he had his heart set on it. I said I could take it or leave it, we could carry on looking. That annoyed B. He said: 'We're moving for your benefit, remember,' which was debatable, though what he meant was that it was close to the school. It is all very tasteful and modern but often I am reminded that it is someone else's idea of perfect living.

While the builder worked away in the bathroom I looked up some things on the Internet. When he was finished he came into the living room and I wrote him a cheque.

'Nice place,' he said.

'It has its disadvantages.'

'Oh?'

'Bit of an insect problem at the moment.'

'Funny time of year for them.'

'Greenfly. We've never had them before.'

'You would've thought you'd be safe from them up here.'

'You would have thought.'

'Perhaps they're attracted by the tropical climate.'

'Perhaps,' I said, and smiled at his joke.

The builder had nodded at the back wall of the living room which was papered with a vast photograph of a jungle scene. The trees were heavy with brightly coloured fruits and parrots and a frothing waterfall tumbled through the middle, the image of a bountiful paradise. This was the one significant addition we had made to the flat, the stamp of our personality. Or B's anyway. It was his idea, I think he'd seen it in a bar he drank in with workpeople. I came home late one evening soon after we moved in, when I was still working, and B intercepted me at the door.

'Close your eyes,' he had said, leading me into the living room. 'OK.'

'Wow,' I said.

'It's kitsch,' B said triumphantly.

'Does that mean the same as ugly?' He looked downcast. 'Joke,' I said.

'Funny,' said B.

That night we took off our clothes and photographed

ourselves posing in front of the scene, draped in garlands of plastic flowers left over from a party. I said I felt like I was in an Elvis movie. B said this was the Garden of Eden and that he had an appetite for some of Eve's forbidden fruit.

By eleven B wasn't home. I went to bed but was still awake when he came in just after twelve. From the amount of noise he was making it was obvious he was drunk. I didn't call out and when he pushed the door of the spare room open I pretended to be asleep. I listened as he clumsily took off his clothes and dropped them on the floor. He got into bed and moved against me.

'Can I stay in here tonight?' he whispered. 'I'm sorry about before, on the phone. I'm under a lot of pressure.' His penis was pushing against my buttock. 'Janey?' He smoothed my hair away from my face. 'Janey?' I lay still. He began to rub gently against me, my back, my buttocks and my thighs, his breaths coming quicker, shallower. His body tensed suddenly, briefly, and he came into the small of my back.

I lay awake listening to B's breathing even out, deepen. When it seemed likely he was asleep I got out of bed, put on my dressing gown and went to the bathroom to shower. Afterwards I went into the kitchen. I drank a glass of water and looked up at the ceiling. It was thick with greenfly. I switched on the light in the living room and saw the same thing. I turned on the computer and waited while it booted up.

I concentrated on the computer screen. I won three games at level five, a good result. My head felt clearer and I shut the computer down and stood up. Standing in the doorway, about to switch off the light, I looked up at the greenfly and had the curious thought that they had been waiting for me, that they came for my benefit. When I thought of this I felt, I suppose, comforted, as if we shared a secret. I even felt a twinge of guilt for vacuuming them up that time.

In the bedroom I slid under the duvet. I couldn't feel them but I knew all against my skin were the greenfly I had deposited there earlier. Still, there were worse things to spend the night with and I wasn't about to put on new sheets at this time.

In the morning I woke to the sound of B slamming the door on his way out to work. I got up and checked each room but there were no open windows so it was really a mystery how they had got in during the night. Nevertheless, the evidence was there, all around, a snowfall of little green bodies. I began the clean-up straight away, still wearing my dressing gown. I hadn't been doing it long when the phone went. It was B, calling from work.

'You haven't forgotten about tonight?' he said. He sounded fragile. 'I'll be home early to cook. Could you,' he said tentatively, 'could you make sure the place is clean?'

'You mean get rid of the greenfly?' There was a pause.

'Sorry, Janey? Someone was talking to me.'

'I said I'm doing it as we speak.'

'Great. I'll see you later.' He hung up.

Martin and Susannah arrived promptly at eight, with a bottle of wine. B had been back for a couple of hours and done all the cooking. At about half past seven he had put the lasagne in the oven and gone into the bedroom to change. When he came out he looked at me and said: 'What are you wearing?' I cocked my head, pretending not to understand. 'Make an effort, Janey,' he said, 'for me?'

'Well, if you put it like that,' I said. In the bedroom I took off the tracksuit bottoms and T-shirt and debated. Finally I put on a skirt and a tight top that B once said was 'whorish, but in a good way'.

B asked me to open the wine while he gave Martin and Susannah 'the tour'. They went out onto the balcony and Martin gave a low whistle when B pointed out how far you could see across the city. In the living room I heard them laugh and when I went in with the wine they were looking at the jungle scene on the back wall. B was grinning inanely. I poured the wine and handed it round.

'Finally, the famous apartment,' said Martin. 'And the famous Janey.'

'The famous Martin,' I said.

'I love your apartment,' said Susannah.

'I tend to think of it as a flat really,' I said.

'Flat, apartment, what's the difference?' said Martin, smiling.

'I've no idea,' I said. 'Perhaps you can tell us?' I turned to B.

'Sit, sit,' he said. 'The food's nearly ready.' We all sat down around the glass coffee table. I was surprised at how similar Martin and Susannah were to how I had expected. She had long blonde hair and I could see she was pretty, in the unimaginative way men find attractive. Martin was reasonably good-looking, as predicted, with what is probably known as a good jaw. He had a cleft in his chin that was like the one Kirk Douglas – and later Michael – has, though the resemblance ended there. B and I often used to talk about couples we knew or who we saw in the street and judge who was the better looking of the pair. Based on the degree of difference we would estimate how long the relationship would last. B and I were usually in agreement. The striking thing about Martin and Susannah was that there was nothing to choose between them – they were exactly as attractive as each other. I wondered if it had occurred to B.

'We're thinking of buying a place round here,' said Susannah, addressing me.

'So I gather,' I said.

'It's on the up, isn't it? Such a mixture of cultures. I love all that. Is it dangerous?'

'Only on the fifth floor,' I said and everyone laughed.

'Martin,' said B, 'come and give me a hand with the food.' B and Martin went into the kitchen.

'Smells amazing,' said Susannah, pronouncing amazing as if it were a very long word.

'More wine?' I said, and filled her glass.

'Martin can just about manage cheese on toast, under supervision. It must be wonderful having a man who can cook.'

'Yes, I'm very lucky,' I said. Susannah got up and walked around the living room, pausing in front of things, touching them. B and Martin came in, each carrying two plates of food.

'Here it is, folks,' said Martin.

'The famous lasagne,' I said.

'Dig in,' said B. We sat down around the dining table and there was no conversation for a while, just the sound of Martin and Susannah murmuring satisfied noises as they ate.

'B says you're a teacher,' Martin said, taking a sip of wine.

I nodded. 'I think you people are amazing. Saints. I could never do it.'

'It's a tough school too,' said B. 'I wouldn't send my kids there.'

'He doesn't mind sending his girlfriend there,' I said, putting a forkful of lasagne into my mouth. Martin chuckled.

'You're not working at the moment though?' said Susannah. I shook my head.

'She's thinking of going back in the new year,' said B.

'What do you do all with all the time?' said Susannah. 'I'd go crazy.' I made a crazy face and Martin and Susannah laughed. B looked uneasy.

'Cheer up,' I said to him, 'the food's not that bad.' Martin and Susannah laughed again. Martin was laughing so much I thought he might slide off his chair, or throw up the lasagne.

'Susannah works in TV,' said B hastily.

'It's funny,' I said. 'I'm always hearing about people who work in TV. Personally I prefer the adverts, more imaginative. Tell me, what do you do in TV?'

'Well, at the moment I'm working on a documentary,' said Susannah. 'Very gritty. Inner-city kids, no prospects, crack addiction and the rest. Give them their own cameras, let them tell their own story.'

'Sounds depressing,' I said.

'You'd be surprised,' said Susannah, 'it's actually great TV.'

'Speaking of TV,' I said, 'I read a story in the paper about a woman who always had the box on at full volume because she was deaf. Eventually it drove her husband mad and he strangled her with the aerial lead.' Martin and Susannah looked at each other. B was looking at his food but not eating it. Martin started laughing first, then Susannah. After that B joined in.

'It worries me how often she tells that story,' said B. It was hard to know what he was talking about because I only just made it up.

Susannah looked around the room. 'I just adore this place. You've done such nice things with it.'

'Oh, that wasn't us,' I said. 'It was all already here. We bought it knockdown from the estate agents. They were only going to trash it otherwise.'

'Please, Martin, can we get one just like it?' she said.

'It's a bit like being trapped in someone else's life,' I said. 'Do you know what I mean?'

'It must be lovely being so close to the water, the canal.'

'Except for the greenfly,' I said.

'Greenfly?' said Susannah.

'Janey seems to think we've been invaded by bugs,' said B.

'Greenfly,' I said. 'They appear every night on the ceiling. In the morning they're dead and I clear them up. Then, at night, they come back. We're infested.'

'Funny time of year for them,' said Martin.

'Isn't it,' I said.

'No sign of them now,' said Susannah, looking up and around.

'Stage fright,' said B, idiotically. 'Janey does like to exaggerate things.'

'Yes,' I said, 'she's always making out things are worse than they are.'

B stood up. 'Janey, come and help me with the dessert.' B and I went into the kitchen and he took some raspberries out of the fridge. He turned towards me and looked like he was about to say something.

'How long do you give them?' I said, before he could speak.

'What?'

'Who's better looking?'

'Janey!' said B. 'They're our guests.'

We went back in with the dessert. It was a pavlova, the other thing B cooked. The meringue was soft in the middle because it hadn't been in the oven for long enough. I had a few mouthfuls and then put my spoon down.

When everyone had finished eating B cleared the plates away and we moved onto the sofa and comfy chairs. Martin said: 'So who'd like a little after-dinner pick-me-up?' and spilled a small mound of cocaine onto the glass table. B said he wouldn't mind at all and Susannah said just a small one for her.

'Janey?' said Martin. B gave me a wary look.

'It doesn't agree with me, Martin,' I said, looking at B. 'Makes me prone to exaggeration.'

After that B, Martin and Susannah talked about their work and people they worked with. Martin said how he already had more money than he knew what to do with and if it kept on like this he could retire in five years. B said it would be miracle if he didn't get a promotion by Christmas. Susannah said how vital she felt her work was because it let people know what was going on beyond their front doors and garden fences. They all agreed with each other very strongly about everything.

I was distracted. I kept looking up at the ceiling. 'Janey,' said Martin, 'it looks like we've lost you. We're telling funny stories about people at work. Tell us something from the world of teaching.' The three of them turned towards me.

'I'm not sure if this counts,' I said, after thinking for a second. 'There was a man I used to teach with. One of his classes locked him in a stationery cupboard. He wept for two hours until someone let him out. His wife had just left him. Three days later I found him hanging from the ceiling of one of the prefabricated classrooms.' B, Martin and Susannah all looked blank, as if I had suddenly started speaking in a foreign language.

'How about some coffee?' said B.

'I'll give you a hand,' said Martin, and they got up and went into the kitchen.

When they had gone Susannah started smiling a funny half-smile, like she had a guilty secret. 'The reason we want a new place,' she said, 'is that we're having a baby. We've known for a little while but we wanted to wait and see if everything was all right. I came from the doctor this evening. You're the first person I've told.'

'You know,' I said, leaning across the table to Susannah, 'B doesn't even believe the greenfly exist.'

B and Martin came back in carrying the coffee and some cups. They were both smiling.

'Martin told me the wonderful news,' B said. He went over to Susannah and kissed her on the cheek. 'Congratulations.'

'You don't mind, do you, baby?' said Martin. Susannah shook her head happily.

'They're having a baby,' B said to me.

'Also known as plant louse or ant cow, they are a species of sap-sucking, soft-bodied insects with tube-like projections known as cornicles on the abdomen. Wingless females produce living young without fertilisation. It can be a serious pest. And yes, it is a funny time of year. I'm guessing global warming has disorientated them. Sudden alterations to a creature's environment can make them act unpredictably or erratically.' B had poured the coffee. He and Susannah were watching Martin divide up three more lines of cocaine. 'If we'd taken the problem seriously to begin with it wouldn't be an issue now,' I went on. 'Still, benefit of hindsight and all that. Of course, B doesn't notice much that's going on around him, he's so focused, obsessive you might say, about his work. Unfortunately poor Janey doesn't have that luxury.' B leaned over the table and snorted the cocaine through a rolled note.

'What was all that, Janey?' he said. Martin and Susannah took their turn leaning over the glass. For a while they talked about what it would be like to have a baby and they all agreed about how exciting it was. Martin mentioned someone at work who had just had a baby and they carried on talking about workpeople, new bars in town, and a holiday Martin and Susannah had taken in the Maldives. At about midnight they got their coats and B walked them to the door.

'I told you it'd be fun.' B had come back into the living room and was massaging my shoulders. His hands felt very rigid and it was quite uncomfortable. 'You were a real hit with them. Martin's suggesting we go down to the cottage the weekend after next.' B stopped massaging, sat down on the sofa and flicked on the TV. 'You know,' he said, not taking his eyes off the screen, 'if I get this promotion you wouldn't have to go back to work at all. You could stay here and have babies.'

I crossed the room and switched on the computer. When it had booted up I played a few games of backgammon. After a while B stood up.

'Right, I'm off to bed,' he said.

'Big day tomorrow?' I said.

'That's it, baby,' said B.

After B had gone I shut down the computer and looked up. It seemed completely normal to see the greenfly there, exposed on the white ceiling, expectant, vigilant, as if they weren't anywhere they shouldn't have been, their shadows flickering in the breeze from the open window.

The Ice Palace

THE TOWN MUSEUM, OPEN ON WEEKDAY AFTERNOONS, HAS two rooms, front and back. In the back room is a scale model of the Ice Palace that was my father's inspiration and built in the town nearly sixty years ago. The once-white card has yellowed and curls at its edges but the intricate detail of the design remains. There are arches, domes, turrets and spires. Colonnaded walkways lead to descending terraces and pavilions. A flag bearing the town's coat of arms is planted on the highest tower. Behind the model rises a gaudily painted diorama of mountains. In front, a number of tiny human figures, standing in groups or alone, look up at the structure with bland, inscrutable expressions. A display board shows a photograph of the palace taken on the day of its completion. The colours have run; the sky is light green, giving the image a fantastical, other-worldly feel. The building itself appears ghostly, insubstantial. The caption reads: *J. P. Graham photograph of the historic Ice Palace built in January 1896 using 5,000 tons of ice. During an early thaw in mid-March of the same year the Ice Palace went the way of all ice.*

I have always liked that: *went the way of all ice.* And I find the card model, limp and discoloured as it is, both sad and beautiful. Perhaps it is the innocence, the absurdity of the idea. Or perhaps the imagination and belief that turned it from idea to reality, however brief. Perhaps it is because of its role in my father's disgrace, but the sight of it, this neglected, wilting monument to a forgotten passion, moves me in ways I cannot understand or explain.

'This town was full of fools,' my mother likes to say. My mother is dying. She is nothing but a bag of bones. The skin of her face is drawn tightly around her skull. Her pale blue eyes are vast in her head. A silver wedding band hangs loose on a frail, liver-spotted finger. Her hair, washed and set every morning at eleven, is candyfloss-thin but sweeps off her scalp in defiantly old-fashioned style. She sits up in her chair and stares out of the window. Her eyes, so different from mine, are the colour of the mountain skies. 'This town was full of fools,' she says, 'and your father was the biggest fool of all.'

One hundred years ago there was no town here. There was nothing but the extreme cold, almost perennial snow, the barren and infertile mountainsides. Above the treeline there was no wood to burn or grass for cattle to eat. Only fugitives and herds of wandering elk were familiar with the inhospitable terrain. But in 1870, the books tell us, the Reverend Kester Swann, a defrocked clergyman, was searching for rare heathers in the mountains. In a gale he was thrown to the ground and found his nose pressed against the cool, hard surface of silver ore.

Thousands of fortune-seekers descended on the unlikely valley to claim the spoils. A town sprang up. The mountainsides were soon littered with mine entrances, joists and slag heaps. Roads connected the town to the east, the west, the north and south of the country. An extraordinary mountain railway that would link the town to the far coasts was soon under construction. Many got rich. My father, who had been scraping a living as a tenant farmer in the east, but who had always imagined such wealth to be his fate, was one of them.

'You've never seen such arrogance,' says my mother. 'Every chancer and crook in the country came to live here. They competed with each other to build the largest, the most vulgar houses. Houses they imagined filling with their heirs. Houses so big they could shit in a different toilet every day of the week. They had their clothes made in London. They smoked Turkish tobacco. They built monuments celebrating their achievements. Their vanity was endless.'

Among my mother's few possessions is a photograph of my father. It shows him in 1888, already a rich man, in high leather boots and a thick fur coat. He is pictured against a snowy mountainside with two other similarly attired men, holding the deeds to the claim that made his fortune. He is smiling and his free hand is held out wide in some grand gesture, the meaning of which is long forgotten. 'A man of appetites,' my mother has called him, her voice spikily suggestive, and I permit myself, despite the murky resolution, to see in the forward angle of his posture, the hook of the nose that is his legacy to me, and the unruly twist of his hair, the energy and folly of his character.

As the town's wealth grew, so too did its infamy. Along with the mansions there were dance halls, gambling houses, theatres and brothels. It was said that the place catered to every kind of sinner. And it was true; these newly rich men gratified themselves fully and indiscriminately. They believed that wealth bought exemption from the prudery and puritanism of the day. For twenty-five years the town boomed and made no apologies for itself. Then, in 1894, the one fragile resource upon which it was all based, the hard, cold, dullish silver extracted from the unprepossessing, long-ignored mountains, ran out.

My mother is bitter. Bitter about her situation, her helplessness and dependency, bitter to be dying. She is rude to the staff here, robust, kindly girls. She curses them for their clumsiness or stupidity. She complains that the food they serve is too hot or too cold. She complains that her room is dirty though her eyes are too poor to tell.

But at other times, when I sit beside her bed, she is only serene. Oblivious to my presence she relives moments of the past aloud and in vivid detail – the surprising warmth of a winter sun on her arm, the smell at dusk of the silver-smelting factories on the edge of the town. Her voice, as she describes these memories to no one, is tender, girlish, and it is possible to imagine how she loved, even still loves, my father. These memories seem to give her peace and she drifts into silence and then sleep. I sit for a while and then stand and unhook the fingers that are curled tightly around my hand.

I picture my father standing on the opera-house stage in 1895. A spotlight picks out the elaborately designed model sitting on a dais. His eyes seem to blaze as he addresses the hushed audience of anxious silver tycoons. Such constructions, he tells them, have been built in countries in the far north. People had travelled hundreds of miles and across borders to witness the phenomena. Five thousand tons of ice – one resource, he boldly joked, that they could be certain would not abandon them – would be sculpted into a full-size replica of what they saw before them. Within the palace would be a winter carnival to rival a world fair.

He already had engineers and architects on hand to make it a reality.

'It was absurd,' my mother says, 'but they were putty in his hands. They had believed they were untouchable. They had persuaded themselves that it was their own talents and abilities, even genius, that had got them this far. They had forgotten that it was only luck and the generosity of the earth that had made them rich.' Indeed, some in the town said this catastrophe was proof that the land could not be treated with such carelessness, such contempt. The pious whispered darkly of hubris and divine judgement. They pointed righteously to those inhabitants of the town who had not got rich, who had laboured in the appalling conditions of the mines and suffered crippling injuries or died early wretched deaths because of their poisoned lungs. 'They were as bewildered as children,' says my mother, 'and they wanted to believe that someone, something, could save them.'

I imagine how my father flatters and cajoles his audience as he speaks. He tells them that tourism is an industry of the future. He tells them that he was once a peasant and that by seizing his opportunities he has become rich. He tells them that he is a man of progress and imagination and he believes that they are too. He insists that the Ice Palace, while extraordinary, is symbolic of something greater, is more than just a palace built of ice.

I think of my father's dramatic statements, the rough emotion of his voice, that of a man not born to wealth. And I fancy I hear something else in his voice, in his choice of words – something coloured by hindsight perhaps, and a lifetime of wondering – the passion for an idea that can only mean one thing. My mother puts it another way. 'There was only one explanation for your father's foolishness,' she says. 'He was in love.'

There is nothing new, unusual or edifying about the story. No photographs of the woman exist but she was young of course, barely a woman, and beautiful, it was said, in the style of her trade. Town folklore has it that she was dark-skinned and thick-haired, as if that were further confirmation of her type. There is dispute about her name. Newspaper reports from my father's trial gave it as one thing but she went by something different, something showy, something cheap. She had arrived, like everyone in the town, from somewhere else. She was poor, no doubt, and hopeful for a better life.

My father was in early middle age. He believed in indulging his desires. The circumstances and manner of their meeting are not hard to guess. My father was not discreet but his peers did not condemn him. After all, it was hardly a town of saints. Some may even have said privately that it was understandable; ten years of marriage and my mother had not given him a child.

In thinking about this woman I have looked for explanations or clues to my father's behaviour. I have wondered what was particular about her to inspire such fervour. What, beyond the tawdry clichés – the heavy perfumes, the rehearsed compliments and easy pleasures – caused him to abandon himself to this doomed ideal? Was it more than a bloated ego that saw no end to what it was entitled to, more than a man stupefied by a professionally compliant mind and body?

Perhaps there is little point in imagining my father's feelings; they were no doubt of the generic kind. Nevertheless

I am curious to know his thoughts as he watched an army of men at work hauling blocks up the mountainside in creation of this bizarre and audacious totem of his ardour. What fantasies were nurtured as the blocks were placed one on top of the other and the glistening walls rose steadily from the ground? What strange expression of his infatuation with this faceless woman did he see in the vaulting arches, the smooth domes, the fragile turrets jutting up into the chill air? The woman herself remains invisible. Whether she was flattered or appalled by the erection of this monument designed to woo her is not known. Whether, impressed with the virility of my father's intentions, she returned his feelings, I can do no more than guess.

Meanwhile the town regained its old bullishness. The tycoons, once more in love with themselves, conspired in my father's courtship and the Ice Palace began to take shape. My father was hailed as a visionary, the saviour of the town. Moves were made to rename the opera house in his honour.

My mother is sleeping. I place my hand lightly on her chest to feel the faint rise and fall of her breathing. The breaths that she takes in are brief, shallow, her exhalations slow and never-ending; it seems that the air is gradually leaving her body.

I have always felt the burden of my mother's love. Maybe it is because I have no brothers or sisters or maybe because of my father's abandonment and later death, but her love has been fierce and absolute, an intensity that has sometimes troubled me and which I have not always known how to return. As a child I found her embraces smothering, her kisses hard and desperate, as if she feared that I would be taken from her, as if her love for me were in doubt. I remember once, when I was a child of seven or eight and playing in the street in the evening, she rushed suddenly from the house and wrapped her arms around me. She was shaking. I feared she might crush the life from my body.

This love has, I sometimes think, even now I am old myself, made a child of me. Perhaps it is because of this love that I have never left this town that everybody leaves. Perhaps that is why I am here, sitting by my mother's bedside, terrified and euphoric, waiting for her death.

Even before the symbolic last block of ice was laid at the opening ceremony the edges of the walls and the tops of the towers had begun to lose their definition. The ice had taken on a slippery, translucent glow, like a weak sun shining through clouds. Inside, water dripped from the grand hall and formed pools on the ground.

Within a few days every edge had become smoothly rounded. Cracks appeared in the domes and the arches began to sag. The terraces were gradually transformed into ragged slopes, pavilions into slushy lakes. Each meticulously designed feature merged into the melting whole and five thousand tons of ice began to work its way remorselessly to the ground. The carnival was abandoned. No visitor ever entered the building.

The tycoons, the investors, appeared every day to watch their money curdle before their eyes. Day after day they watched in silence, compelled, their expressions dumb with the impossibility of what they were seeing. The rest of the town turned out too, along with the curious from further afield, to witness the spectacle. The sun was shining. The mountains were raw and beautiful. Children played in the slush. It was an event and the town was once more notorious. It was not the event they had been led to expect.

At the beginning of the third week the highest tower began to lean precariously forward. Two days later it finally toppled over, burying the town flag beneath it. Within a month the palace was simply one more hump of melting ice, on a mountainside covered with them.

'It was ridiculous from the beginning,' my mother says. 'A woman would have seen that. It was the kind of vanity that men always mistake for passion or imagination.' At first the investors told themselves they had been unlucky with the unseasonably early thaw. Then they blamed the engineers and architects for their lack of expertise and sloppy approach. But soon they settled on the figure of my father. It was, after all, his conviction, his delusion, that had led to it being built.

The pious – vindicated once more – were quick to point out that this was a mining town, a town built on solid things, things of reliable worth, things you could hold in your hand. How had they, the wealthy, the foolish, allowed themselves to be seduced by something as ephemeral as ice? They had invested in good faith, they replied. They had not known my father was a charlatan. Had anyone, besides him, ever heard of such a thing, a palace built out of ice? He was a charlatan. He was a charlatan besotted with a whore.

It is not known what effect the sight of the Ice Palace ebbing away had on my father. What is known is that the woman to whom this grand gesture was directed disappeared abruptly from the town. The common assumption was that after my father's public disgrace and bankruptcy she saw no reason to stay, a view in line with her supposedly fickle nature and the habits of her profession. I have entertained other possibilities. Had his failure caused his feelings for her to wane? Or hers for him? Had the melting absurdity of the Ice Palace shown to him the frailty of his passion? The two had after all been linked – confused even – in his mind. I have entertained other possibilities, too.

My father was tried and convicted of fraud by a court and a town desperate to purge the memory of their mistake. A picture in the newspaper on the day of his release from jail shows a changed man. He was thin now and stooped, his face deeply lined, no longer the swashbuckling entrepreneur pictured on the snowy mountainside a decade before. While he was in jail my mother and father had been reconciled. But there was to be no domestic bliss. Once he was released he drank and took to morose wanderings around the sites of his old claims. In March 1900, barely four years after his conviction, he was found dead at the bottom of a mine shaft, apparently having fallen down one of the poorly marked holes. Many suggested something more premeditated.

My mother has no harsh words for the woman whom my father abandoned her for. 'She was just a girl', she says, 'just a girl', and when she says this I feel that there is a message for me, a plea for understanding. But she volunteers no more and I do not have the heart, the courage, to press her.

Our town is mentioned in guidebooks to the region. It is one feature of a scenic driving tour which includes a reservoir and a dam named after a president. The books insist that you witness the dilapidated grandeur of the mansions, the theatres and the baroque churches that front half a mile of our main street. From my mother's room I have watched the cars slow to allow passengers to peer out of the windows. Perhaps one will be reading aloud a condensed history of the town or pointing out things of particular interest, the venue, say, of a notorious shooting or scandal. Soon the once-elegant facades falter and then cease. The books draw attention to the last building worthy of note – a former brothel, now a run-down travellers' hostel – and the cars accelerate away. I imagine that little is said as the cars wind their way through the landscape of slag heaps that have taken root as hills. Back on the highway talk turns to the next destination. Little impression of our town remains, except an unacknowledged gladness for the warmth, the motion of the vehicle, and a trace of unease at the memory of neglect, the near empty streets.

My mother has become weaker still, though it hardly seems possible. She is no longer comfortable sitting up in her chair. Instead, she lies in bed, her shoulders and head supported on a pile of cushions. If I am there at mealtimes the staff are grateful if I feed her. Her appetite is good but it is an effort for her to eat. She is silent now, as if she has said all she wants, all she needs. She can do almost nothing for herself and I am made to think of myself as an awkward, bawling infant, dependent on the unconditional love and nurturing of others.

When she is no longer hungry she leans her head back and her eyes turn unfocused towards the window. Looking at her I am forced to contemplate, yet again, the sudden departure of the woman of whom no pictures remain. I wonder at the terms of the reconciliation between my mother and father that, I am told, brought me into the world. I am compelled to imagine the circumstances of my birth and I fantasise a Gothic scene, something from the storybooks:

a new-born infant swaddled in blankets, a clandestine meeting between two women, one of them ten years without a child, the other barely more than a child herself.

I return also to the image of the Ice Palace in 1896. Like my father's lover no pictures record its demise; even as they watched, unable to turn away, they knew they would soon wish to forget. So I am forced to imagine the rounded walls and turrets, the slow-motion collapse of the domes and the arches, the toppling tower, and I see in all this some strange and distant imprint of myself. Incongruous, bizarre, a manifestation of arrogance and greed. And yet still, for me, it remains eerily beautiful, perfect, sufficient to itself.

My mother has drifted off again still propped up on cushions, the gap between the world and sleep now so thin. I tidy her lunch away and tuck the blankets in around her. Her head has rolled to one side as if she were offering me her cheek. When I lean down to kiss her goodbye her skin is soft, always so unexpectedly soft, like a child's.

The Good Guy

WHEN HE WAS TWENTY-EIGHT AND LONELY, JP BEGAN A relationship with a woman over email. Her name was Molly. An old friend of his, Roland, had met her in a bar and at the end of the night he had given her JP's email address instead of his own. The following day Roland called to suggest that he play along but JP wanted no part in the prank (which was typical Roland). When an email came a few days later he put Molly straight immediately. She replied that she was very embarrassed and appreciated his honesty, and her tone was so pleasant and unassuming – not at all like the kind of woman he imagined being chatted up by his friends in a bar – that he wrote to her again. He told her that she wasn't to worry or feel like she had been made a fool of, because as far as he was concerned she hadn't. She replied again, saying how thoughtful he seemed, and kind. Soon they were emailing every day.

The relationship came at a good time for JP. He had finished his PhD the previous year – a 100,000-word study, 'Death and The Dead in the fiction of James Joyce', which made him feel ill every time he thought about it – and had just begun his first teaching job in a town where he knew no one and which was continually wet and tormented by a biting North Sea wind. JP felt like a fraud. Every day he stood terrified in front of his students who, with their confidence and frank sexuality, seemed to know more about life than he was ever likely to. When he discussed Leopold Bloom's mastur-bation he found himself blushing uncontrollably.

The university campus was a maze of buildings, squares and high walkways that seemed to have been cut out of one vast piece of concrete. According to the university's promotional material it was designed on the model of an Italian hill village. This, JP concluded, was either a cruel or absurd joke. A fashionable prejudice against windowsills at the time it was built meant that rain ran uninterrupted down the side of the buildings leaving great damp stains. The wind came off the sea, got up speed across the East Anglian plains and funnelled itself around the buildings. Making his way about campus, JP would sometimes find himself pushed off balance or spun round by an unexpected pocket of turbu-lence. And it was at these times, or as he made his way to or from a lecture along one of the stilted walkways, the rain seeming to drive into him from the side rather than above, that his whole future would stretch out in front of him like a bleak and featureless landscape . . .

This was not all. Three months after he started the new job, JP had the first of what he began privately to call his 'turns'. It happened as he was sitting in his office, waiting to go and deliver a lecture. He stood up to pull a book off the shelf and the floor seemed to roll under him, like the deck of a ship. He held onto the bookshelf with both hands to stop himself falling. There was a tightness across his chest, he could not catch his breath, and for several minutes he wondered if he was having a heart attack. But it soon passed and he was able to make it to the lecture on time.

Two weeks later he was watching a film in an almost empty cinema when he was gripped by a powerful claustrophobia.

He rushed out into the street and sat on the freezing pavement, panting for air.

'Panic attack,' said the campus GP. 'You're part of a growing statistic.' JP did not know whether he was supposed to be reassured by this. 'I could tell you what's happening physiologically,' said the doctor, waving a hand dismissively, 'but personally I feel that this is an *existential* rather than a *medical* phenomenon. One for the philosophers, perhaps?' He smiled briefly at JP and then spun back to face his computer screen. 'Don't get me wrong. I'm glad you came in. I'll put you down for some counselling.'

'Am I dying?' JP had no idea where the question had come from.

The doctor did not look round. 'We're all *dying*,' he said.

And then, towards the end of the first winter, came the email from Molly. She was American, from Chicago, and had been on business in London when she met Roland. At thirty-five she was a few years older than JP and had, as she put it, 'nearly been married a couple of times'. She told him she had been named after Molly Bloom and this seemed to JP such a wondrous coincidence that he could not help but see it as some kind of omen. Very quickly he shared his anxieties about his work with her. 'I don't have anything useful to teach anyone,' he wrote. 'Sometimes when I'm standing there, I feel so insubstantial, as if you could reach out and put your hand right through me.' She replied that she didn't know much about literature but that it seemed wonderful to take such a small thing and give it so much attention. 'If everyone did what I did' – something to do with investment funds that JP did not try too hard to understand – 'then the world wouldn't be much of a place.'

Although she had sent him a picture of herself (short dark hair, a small mouth, very pale blue eyes), when he thought of her he did not picture a person so much as a kind of light, a beacon in a dismal sea. The sense of quiet dread that had hung around him all year began to lift. His teaching improved; he felt perhaps there was something here after all and that he might have access to it. Leopold Bloom's masturbation no longer brought forth his blushes. The panic attacks were rarer and he learned to breathe his way through them.

Gradually the emails became more intimate. JP was honest, if not specific, about his lack of experience (a handful of one-night stands and a fraught and almost entirely chaste fling with a fellow Joyce scholar) but this did not seem to affect Molly's interest. And although JP had never been comfortable or confident with sexual matters, over email he did not feel the usual inhibitions. After some prompting from Molly he sent her a message describing what he thought it would be like to go to bed with her. In return she explained in detail some of the things she would do to him when they met. She had been reading Molly Bloom's soliloquy and quoted it at him: 'No I never in all my life felt anyone had one the size of that to make you feel full up.' None of this seemed tasteless or risky, only intensely erotic.

Then, abruptly, the emails stopped. At first JP could not understand it. He read and reread the last of her messages but there had been no warning, no disagreement or cooling in their tone. Molly had been talking about a trip to London she was going to have to take and at which they had planned to meet. At first he was genuinely concerned; he believed that something must have happened to her. But then the emails he sent began to be returned to him – the address she had been using had been closed down – and he quickly saw the way things were. He understood now that she had never intended that things would go further or that they would ever meet, that it had been some sort of game. What had been a source of private comfort, even joy, became a private misery and he was left feeling even lower than before.

At the end of the summer Roland called to say that he was getting married and to ask if JP would be his best man. It caught JP by surprise. He had heard Roland mention his girlfriend, Larissa, before but he had never met her and had not guessed it was serious. More than this though, he felt sure that Roland had other, better friends who could perform this duty. After all, they spoke on the phone from time to time but had not seen each other in more than a year. 'Don't worry about a stag do,' Roland said, 'just show up for the weekend.'

JP had sat next to Roland at his first lecture on his first day at university and they had become unlikely friends. JP was used to being ignored or patronised by a certain sort of person but here the differences between them – Roland's brashness and hedonism versus JP's nerviness and reserve – made them something of a double act. They found each other exotic, JP thought, and redeemed each other a little. Roland, for his part, regarded JP as a great wit and eccentric. 'You're funny,' he said, 'you have humour,' and he would introduce JP to his friends as 'the oddest guy I know'. Gradually JP played up to this role, becoming excessively dry, cautious, cynical. It became part of their routine that JP would make friends with girls that Roland wanted to sleep with, a kind of unthreatening bait. 'The Trojan Horse,' Roland called him, and though for a time he felt some reflected glory in Roland's conquests he later began to recognise it as a humiliation. As time went on he saw that he had made too much of a pet of himself and when, at the end of their degree, Roland went to work in the City and JP stayed on to do his master's, he was not unhappy to be free of these expectations.

Since then the friendship had faded. But now, after the initial surprise, JP began to see things in a different light. Perhaps he had underestimated Roland, himself, what was between them. He began to look forward to the wedding and, months later, as he sat on the train to the West Country, his anxieties were balanced by a new hopefulness. It was spring and this feeling was echoed in the greenness of the hedgerows rushing past the window. Things happen at weddings, he thought. Who knew what might happen?

At the station Roland hugged JP and then held him at arm's length, a hand on each of JP's shoulders. 'Hombre!' he said. 'Looking a little fragile, if you don't mind me saying. Modern life getting to you?'

'I'm dying,' said JP.

Roland slapped him on the back. 'Nice one. Well, don't do it before the end of the weekend. That would be *muy inconveniente.*' Roland did not look so good himself, JP thought. He appeared not to have slept. He smelled faintly sour. There were little white crusts of spittle at the corners of his mouth and the pores of his nose were swollen and raw.

Roland drove fast down the country lanes, his left hand hovering over the horn. 'You know, JP,' he said, 'I recommend marriage, I really do. I know, I know. You're thinking, "He's not even married yet and already he's the world expert." But seriously, it's going to make me a better person. I can feel it.'

'How?' said JP. Roland was staring ahead at the road, suddenly deep in thought. He wiped something from his lip and turned to JP.

'Anyway. Look at me, lecturing you. How are things in academia?' Roland pronounced the word slowly as if it were both grand and slightly foolish, like you might say 'diplodocus', JP thought. But he did not get the chance to reply. Roland leaned heavily on the horn and did not let go for what seemed to JP like a whole minute. 'I'm getting married tomorrow,' he shouted over the noise, apparently addressing no one in particular. 'Can you fucking believe it? I'm getting married tomorrow.'

Ten minutes later they arrived at the house where the wedding was to be held, a Victorian mansion that seemed to extend itself further and further in every direction as they approached along the winding drive. In one corner was a turret that looked like it had been added as an afterthought and did not quite match the style. Vast lawns ran down to a lake. In a meadow below the house a figure on a grey horse made its way over a series of jumps. Roland parked round the back of the building and led JP through the kitchens and up several flights of stairs. At the end of a long oak-panelled corridor lined with gloomy portraits were more stairs. They climbed to the top and Roland opened a door. 'Muchos apologies for the decor,' he said. 'I believe this is billed as the Raj Suite.'

JP could not help but be dismayed. The room was enormous. The high walls were hung with elaborate Indian tapestries in red and gold. At the far end, perhaps ten yards from where JP was standing, a low bed was stacked with cushions and bright silks. There were mahogany chairs, sofas, tables and a dresser. On the floor near the door lay a tiger-skin rug. Beyond it, in a corner, stood a child-sized statue of a native with a garishly painted-on grin, holding out a tray with a teapot. Three tall windows stared down on the gardens and, beyond them, a lake. Through another door two claw-footed baths sat side by side in the bathroom. It would be impossible not to feel inadequate in a room like this, JP thought.

'Think this is obscene, you should see ours,' said Roland. 'Africa!' He sat down in one of the armchairs and pulled something out of his inside jacket pocket. For a moment JP thought Roland was about to offer him drugs. At a party a few years before he had given him some cocaine. Afterwards JP had spoken urgently about his PhD thesis to a girl he had not met before and then thrown up in an alleyway. The following morning he had woken up with a sense of self-loathing so sharp that it was like a physical pain.

Roland took out a bottle of pills and unscrewed the cap. He grinned at JP. 'Not what you're thinking. Only what the doctor gives me these days.' He put two of the pills in his mouth and then went to the bathroom and turned on a tap.

He came back into the room. 'Leave you to settle in, then. Work on your speech or something. Of course we're expecting something special – everyone is.' Roland hugged JP. 'Thanks, hombre. Means a shitload.'

Once Roland had gone, JP took off his shoes and lay on the bed. He closed his eyes so that he would not have to look at the room and thought about the speech he would be making the next day. He had spent every evening for the last month working out what he was going to say. It was all typed neatly onto three-by-five cards which he had numbered and tucked in a zipped pocket inside his bag. But thinking of it now, he could not remember how it began or ended, or anything in between. The words ran together in a blur. All he knew was that it was full of dreadful platitudes and even worse jokes. The thought of standing up in front of a room full of people made his heart race. 'Show love,' someone had told him, 'that's all you need to do.' Show love, he thought. Show love . . .

When he woke, JP felt groggy and disorientated. He had dreamed of standing at the front of a crowded room delivering his speech, naked from the waist down.

In the main hall, the party was in full swing. JP descended the wide, curving staircase slowly, looking out for anyone he knew. It was crammed with people, standing in groups, drinking and laughing. Waitresses in black trousers and white shirts circled the room with trays of champagne and there was an atmosphere of people having an extraordinarily good time. JP stood on his own at the bottom of the stairs, trying not to look conspicuous. He recognised no one. It was confusing – who were all these people, he wondered. He turned to look at the paintings on the wall. The one behind him showed twenty or thirty dogs – beagles, JP thought they were called – racing over a hedge in some kind of frenzied pursuit. The painting was so vast and so comprehensively detailed that every straining muscle of the dogs seemed to rise off the canvas.

JP crossed the hall and went into the kitchens. There was a crowd here too. Two men were sitting side by side at a steel counter, bare-chested, their shirts tied around their heads. Beside each of them was a large pile of bananas which they were unpeeling and eating at great speed, their faces expressions of pure concentration. The crowd were urging them on with monkey noises and the shout 'Eat! Eat!'

JP walked back into the hall and immediately found himself part of a circle of people. They were all laughing wildly. Someone seized JP's arm. A remarkably beautiful woman started to speak. 'So, a black man, a Jew and a dog go into a bar.' Everyone laughed. 'Not really,' said the woman. 'A bear goes into a bar and says: "I'd like a pint of –"' She looked around at the faces watching her and then down at her feet. She sipped her drink slowly. '"– Beer please." Barman says: "Hey, why the big paws?"'

They all whooped and clinked their glasses. 'Look here,' said the man holding JP's arm. He had very thick black-rimmed glasses. 'This is a very important discussion. We're doing a survey to see who has the best joke. When we've heard them all we'll vote. What's your joke?'

They all turned eagerly to JP. His mind was blank. There were jokes in his best man's speech but not that kind. Someone at work had told him a joke the previous week, but he had no memory of how it went or whether or not it had been funny. 'Well,' he began, and they all leaned towards him. At that moment a stream of people surged out of the kitchens and into the hall. The two shirtless men were at the front, their faces monk-like, determined. Behind them came the crowd that had been watching them eat bananas. The crowd had their fists in the air and were chanting 'Swim the lake! Swim the lake!' The cry quickly took hold and a conga line of people began marching across the hall and out of the doors into the gardens. 'Swim the lake!' they shouted. 'Swim the lake!'

The hall emptied. One man lay sleeping on a sofa. JP wondered whether he should look for Roland. He opened the door into a room off the hall. Inside a couple were grappling with each other against a wall. 'Fuck off,' said the woman. JP closed the door. He stood at a window for a few minutes, listening to the shouts coming from the gardens, and then climbed the stairs to his room.

JP woke up several hours later. A lamp was on and Roland was sitting in one of the armchairs, smoking a very large cigar. His face was half in shadow and for a few moments JP wondered if he had woken into another dream, one in which Roland was a gangster come to execute him.

'Hello, hombre. Did I wake you? Can't see the bride on her wedding night. You know the rules.'

There was a line of cocaine on the table in front of him. He nodded at it, almost sorrowfully, JP thought. 'Fancy a toot?'

JP shook his head.

'Didn't think so. Keep me company though?'

'Fine,' said JP and pushed himself up in bed.

Roland leaned over the table and snorted it up. He pinched his left nostril closed and sniffed sharply, then the right.

'Tell me,' he said, wiping the back of his hand across his face. 'Do you ever wonder about things – you know, really wonder? Take Larissa. She's a terrific girl, right, it's just . . .' Roland trailed off. 'I know what you're thinking. You're thinking, spare me the wedding-night nerves, eh, hombre?'

JP did not know what he was thinking. Roland sighed. 'I guess I'm just a little tightly wound right now.' He began to separate out another line. 'I've been having this dream, right, and in this dream I'm trying to run away from someone. I can't get away from them so I end up stabbing them with a knife, and it goes on for ages, really bloody, until I've killed them. I've been having it for months, always the same, and I wake up really freaked. The other day I worked it out. The thing is, I think the person I'm killing is me. What do you make of that?'

Even in the dim light, JP felt the lurking absurdity of the room and its decoration. He pushed himself further up in bed. At the other end of the room he could just see the silhouette of the native.

'I don't know,' said JP, 'it sounds pretty disturbing.' He paused. 'I guess we all have our low moments,' he began. 'I was seeing this woman – well, not exactly seeing, but we had something going. You met her. Molly.'

JP explained what had happened. Roland was quiet but at the end he said, 'But you don't regret it, right? Better to have loved and lost and all that?'

'I don't know,' said JP, 'it hurt a lot.'

Roland snorted the line that had been sitting in front of him.

'JP, let me ask you something. Seriously, I want you to tell me, because I trust you. Am I a cunt? Larissa thinks so. She tells me all the time.'

'No,' said JP, 'I don't think so.'

'Thanks, hombre. I'm glad you said that because I really wanted you to come and do this for me. I don't want to go on about it but I've been having a lot of dreams lately and they seem – I don't know – significant. Anyway, I had a dream about the wedding and you were there, the best man. And when I woke up I knew it was completely right, that the wedding needed you, that you would know exactly what to say. Don't ask me why. I guess I just always thought of you as one of the good guys, that's all.'

He dragged on the cigar and blew great thick smoke rings across the room.

'Anyway,' he said, 'thanks for the little heart-to-heart. It's been good. A load off.' He stubbed the cigar out in an ashtray, stood up and stretched. 'You know the hilarious thing? I didn't even mean to propose. Misunderstanding. Anyway, long story. The day begins. Guess I'll go and see what's happening downstairs.'

After he had gone, JP got out of bed and crossed to the bathroom. There he ran a searingly hot bath and then sat in it, watching the sky lighten outside until the water went cold.

Later, JP went out. He went down to the lake and then walked around it, watching water spurt from the fountain in the middle. On one side of the lake was a maze, a stone lion on either side of the entrance. He went in. He remembered being told as a child that if you hugged the left-hand wall wherever it went then you would always find your way to the centre. It seemed odd to JP that every maze would conform to this rule but he tried it and, after ten minutes, he arrived in the middle. There was a bench with initials and dates etched deeply into it, and a cherry tree just beginning to bud. He lay on the bench. He could see water from the fountain high in the air and imagined he could feel its spray on his face. Somewhere else in the maze there were voices. JP fell into a doze and when he woke two things had come clearly into his head. The first was that Roland had written the emails – there never had been a Molly. The second was the joke he had been told at work.

JP hardly noticed the wedding ceremony. He stood at the front of the main hall next to Roland. When Larissa came down the stairs in her dress, JP registered her vaguely as the girl he had thought to be Molly – the short dark hair, small mouth and pale blue eyes of the picture. Roland and Larissa read their vows, JP produced the ring from his pocket and they signed the marriage register. At the end of the ceremony the guests sang a song which they all seemed to know but which JP did not recognise.

Lunch was in the dining room. JP was on the top table with Roland and Larissa's family. Each person's place was marked with a little clue or riddle written on a piece of ornately designed card. JP's said 'The Trojan Horse'. Next to him was one of the men who had gone to swim the lake. He was Larissa's brother. Several people called out to him with monkey noises and mimed eating a banana, and he did the same back to them.

'Was it cold?' asked JP.

The brother looked blankly at him.

'The water. Was the lake cold?'

The brother shrugged and turned to speak to someone else.

JP picked at his food. The room was noisy and hot, and he felt extremely tired. A microphone was set up at one end of the room and after lunch the speeches began. Each time JP thought he was about to be announced, someone else stood up. An uncle of Roland's delivered a whole speech in rhyming couplets, a novelty that brought the house down. JP wondered if Roland had dreamed of every single one of these people speaking at his wedding. When the fourth person, Larissa's mother, stood up, JP went out to use the toilet. He stood leaning against the wall, taking deep breaths. Then he sat on the toilet and emptied his bowels. When he got back the room was quiet, and Larissa's mother was sitting down.

JP walked the length of the room to the microphone.

Everyone was staring at him. Roland was smiling but his face was stretched, tense. JP noticed the man from the night before with the black-rimmed spectacles, the couple grappling behind the door, the man sleeping on the sofa. He had the sudden, strong sensation that they knew all his secrets, everything there was to know about him – but this did not seem so bad. He felt light, powerful.

When he reached the microphone JP took out the speech cards from his jacket. His hands were sweaty and as he brought the cards up to his face he fumbled them and they fell to the floor. 'Oh,' said someone. JP was about to kneel down to gather them up when the thought hit him. He did not need them. He had a great deal to say – it would just be a question of knowing where to start. He cleared his throat.

Just then, JP felt his chest tighten. The floor rocked abruptly under him. He knew what was happening and he reached out to steady himself on a table. One of the guests laughed, then another; there was a smattering of applause. 'Speech!' shouted someone. 'Speech!' and a cry went up. 'Speech! Speech!'

'I'm not –' began JP and then slid to the floor . . .

When his eyes opened, JP felt a new clarity. People were gathered round him on all sides. 'Hombre!' said Roland. Between the crush of bodies JP spotted an open window on the far side of the room and began to make his way towards it. He felt as if he were floating free of his body. 'Show love,' he cried out ecstatically. 'Show love.' Roland was coming after him. He did not look well, JP thought, not at all well. 'Hombre!' called Roland but his voice already seemed very far away. JP went on towards the window and the open air beyond.

Mrs Echegary

IF HE COULD NOT MAKE IT, HE ALWAYS CALLED. OFTEN IT WAS because of his work, sometimes because of his wife or children. 'You're not angry?' he'd ask. 'No,' she'd say, and she was not angry. She was very understanding, she knew the pressures and difficulties of their arrangement. 'Next time,' he'd say, 'I promise.' On these days she did not leave immediately. She listened to opera on the radio, watched television or read magazines. She did not like to think that she was simply waiting for Jorge.

They had been meeting at the Hotel Mirabelle – Jorge and Luisa – twice a week, Mondays and Fridays, for eight months. Today, as always, she got there a little early; there were things to do before Jorge arrived. At the reception desk the manager came out to greet her. The first time she had come in he had recognised her, said he was a big fan, and she had signed in not as herself but as *Mrs Echegary*. The manager had liked the joke and she had done the same thing each time since. Now he watched her hands while she wrote in the book and he smiled, a smile that said he knew how to be discreet, assured her, once again, that it was that kind of hotel. He was young, she thought, almost handsome. He passed her the room key and she winked at him, a showy wink she had been using for years.

Upstairs she made herself a drink, whisky with a little water, and undressed in front of the full-length mirror. She applied more mascara and lipstick quickly, expertly. She brushed her hair and then sprayed perfume around her shoulders and between her legs. She pulled at the skin of her neck and watched it regain its shape. Luisa held her breasts in her hands, enjoying the new, still unexpected weight of them. For a second, in front of the mirror, she arched her spine and tilted her head back.

At the window she adjusted the blinds so that the sunlight lay in bands across the bed. There was something about meeting in this shady room in the bright, dead hours of the afternoon, something deliciously illicit that she thought she must be addicted to. Satisfied, she lit one of her vanilla-flavoured cigarillos and got into bed.

This was how Jorge liked it to be when he arrived. This, he said, was the thought that made him drive a little too fast across the city to the Hotel Mirabelle.

The operation was Jorge's idea. It was their six-month anniversary and he said he wanted to buy her something special. The surgeon was a friend of his, his golf or tennis partner. Jorge made all the arrangements and went with her to the consultation at the clinic. There the two men and Luisa discussed the shape and size of the implants and Jorge paid in advance.

The day of the operation Jorge had been unable to be there because of his work. 'Felipe will look after you,' he told Luisa on the phone. The surgeon explained everything slowly and in detail, where the incisions would be made and how the implants would be inserted. He felt that she should understand exactly what would be happening to her. She listened to the pleasant, almost hypnotic sound of his voice but not to what he was saying. He made her hold the implants in her hands – cool, formless – and she could not connect them with the operation she was about to have.

The surgeon put her at ease. He had something of Jorge's confident, relaxed manner. He said he and his wife had been watching her for years, that his daughter wanted to be an actress, but then didn't they all? He was concerned that she would end up disappointed. Luisa watched him spread the plastic surgical sheet over her and thought that it would not be so different from being touched by Jorge. 'Yes,' she said, 'it is a difficult business. I have been lucky.' She had been about to say something more but the anaesthetic had taken her under.

At their next meeting she was very sore – she had not expected to be so sore – but Jorge was very understanding. He said it made him happy just to look at her.

Luisa picked up the phone and called downstairs for a bottle of champagne, the Veuve Clicquot she and Jorge always drank. She sat at the dressing table in her negligee and began to paint her toenails a bright red.

Built into one corner of the room was a bar with a Formica counter. A mock chandelier hung from the centre of the ceiling. On two walls there were reproductions of Toulouse-Lautrec paintings. From the window there was a view of the hotel car park. Over the last few months the room had become extraordinarily familiar but she rarely allowed herself to think of it, or of Jorge, when she was not here. It was a fragile pleasure, hoarded away at the back of her mind, where she could be sure it would not escape or be used up.

She did not recognise the maid who brought up the champagne and she stopped painting her nails to look. The girl was slim and dark and her hair was pinned flat on top of her head. She was wearing the hotel's black-and-white uniform and black lace-up shoes.

'Where would you like the champagne, Mrs Echegary?'

Luisa pointed towards the bar with the nail brush. 'What is your name?' she asked.

'Mariana.' The maid took the bottle and two glasses off the tray.

'Are you new, Mariana?'

'I've been here for nearly a year, Mrs Echegary.'

Luisa beckoned her over to the dressing table.

'Tell me what you think of this colour. Is it too much?'

'It's very nice, Mrs Echegary.'

Luisa smiled. She wanted to say: You know Mrs Echegary is not my real name? You understand the joke? She said: 'But it doesn't really matter what we think, does it?'

The maid shook her head. She picked up the tray and turned towards the door.

'Wait,' said Luisa. She went to her bag and pulled out her purse. 'How old are you, Mariana?'

'Nineteen.'

Luisa pushed a note into her hand. 'Don't say anything. I'm feeling extravagant.'

Aventuras del Corazon. She wondered how many televisions in the hotel were showing the soap opera now, the first episode of the day, if perhaps the manager was watching it in his office. *Mrs Echegary*: a household name, a national institution according to some. Passionate and ruthless, famous for her diamonds, her perfect hair, her immaculate appearance maintained whatever the circumstances. She had survived the death of two husbands, the delinquency of her sons, cancer and several car crashes.

Luisa put down the remote control without turning the television on, walked to the window and parted the slats of the blind to look out over the hotel car park. She had a momentary vision of herself from the other side of the room – holding the tall glass, the light streaming across her face – as if caught in a photograph or a painting, and she felt a terrifying instant of paralysis. She stood a little straighter to break the thought, and took a sip of champagne.

The car park was quiet. The parking valet was sitting on the kerb, shining his sunglasses with a handkerchief. In the far corner her Alfa Romeo was half hidden by a Mercedes jeep. She had had the car imported from Italy ten years ago at a time when she had left *Aventuras del Corazon* and just received admiring reviews for a role in an American film. The magazines carried photographs of her driving it around the city or filling it with petrol at garages. The car was a little battered and rusting now but there was a powerful sentimentality that stopped her replacing it. Recently the door on the driver's side had broken and she had to get in through the passenger door, sliding awkwardly over the gearstick. It occurred to her again that she should get it fixed.

Three weeks ago Luisa saw Jorge in the Mall Mariscal Lopez. After the party where they had met and the consultation at the clinic it was only the third time she had seen him outside the room in the hotel. He was with two children, a boy and a girl, buying them drinks and hamburgers. They did not look like him, were pale where he was dark. They resembled their mother, Luisa presumed. Looking at them she had no idea how old they might be; Jorge had never said. It occurred to her that in some way she had doubted that they, or his wife, really existed, but were just figments of a game Jorge and Luisa played out in the Hotel Mirabelle.

The food the children had been waiting for was handed over the counter and the three of them turned and began to walk towards Luisa. Jorge appeared somehow different. Unshaven, casually dressed and loaded down with shopping bags, he seemed reduced, crumpled, physically shorter even. As they came closer she saw that he was wearing his wedding ring. Months before, as they were being introduced, she had searched his hand for the ring and not found it.

Jorge and his children were no more than ten feet away and she was preparing to speak to him, when she realised that he had not seen her. They walked past and his face registered nothing, except a certain weariness. She turned to watch them go and as they went he stooped down and said something to the children that made them giggle. A few moments later Luisa realised that a young woman was touching her sleeve and saying her name. She was asking for an autograph and Luisa was happy to be distracted by the ritual.

The next day was a Monday and in the afternoon Jorge and Luisa met in the room at the Hotel Mirabelle. She did not mention the mall. It was a month since Luisa's operation but she was still too uncomfortable to have sex. Jorge had seemed tense but they drank and later he knelt beside her on the bed and masturbated over her breasts.

The champagne was finished. She would order more for her and Jorge later. Instead she poured herself another whisky. The stripes of sunlight coming through the blinds were softer now and had climbed up against the wall.

Luisa turned on the television. The second of the

consecutive episodes of *Aventuras del Corazon* had just begun. The programme seemed to be full of the new young stars whom she barely knew but whose faces were always in the newspapers, their frantic and scandalous personal lives reported in endless detail.

Luisa disliked it when she heard other actors say that they could not bear to see themselves on the screen; she believed it was a pose, an affectation. She enjoyed watching herself in this role, which, after so many years – and despite the dull and insubstantial storylines she felt Mrs Echegary had recently been given – fitted her like a second skin.

Two years after Luisa left the programme she had come back. In that time she made several films but the moment had quickly passed and the parts were no longer offered. Mrs Echegary, who had been killed by a jealous lover in front of an audience of millions – so adamant had Luisa been that she would not return – was resurrected, as feisty and indomitable as before.

Luisa lit another cigarillo and watched the smoke hang heavily above the bed. She picked up the phone and listened to the dreary, insistent hum of the dial tone. When she finally looked back at the television the credits were scrolling up the screen.

'I'd like another bottle of Veuve Clicquot.'

'Of course, Mrs Echegary.' Luisa put down the phone. She wondered if she had heard a different, perhaps a mocking emphasis in the manager's voice.

In the bathroom she turned on the taps. Jorge would be surprised to find her in the bath, Luisa thought. Surprised and a little amused, the way he sometimes was.

Today was Friday and on Monday they had slept together

for the first time since the operation six weeks ago. They had had sex twice and then lay in bed drinking and talking for the rest of the afternoon. Jorge told her that as a teenager he had fantasised about her, something he had never said before. Luisa told him about the house she planned to buy in the mountains which they would be able to use for their meetings. He told her how unhappy he was with his wife and they made love again.

The phone was ringing. If he could not make it, he always called. She did not hurry from the bathroom. She turned off the taps and as she passed the mirror she paused to move a strand of hair away from her face.

'Yes?'

'Mrs Echegary?'

'Yes?'

'I'm afraid there is no more Veuve Clicquot. Only Moët. It is a little cheaper. Mrs Echegary?'

'Yes,' said Luisa, 'please send it up.'

She turned on the hot tap and let it run until the water was steaming. Then, without testing it, she stepped quickly in. For several seconds she felt nothing, there was no sensation. Then the pain came, biting exquisitely. But she did not get out. Instead she lowered herself into the water, feeling the skin tighten and become raw as it hit the water.

She gasped out loud and thought, I can tolerate this.

She counted slowly to twenty, looking at her hands, red under the water. Then she turned the cold tap on and let the bath fill.

The operation had been painful too. There were only scars now, deep red lines etched into the skin which would not disappear, but they were concealed on the undersides. She saw that it was nothing really. Many women she knew, especially in her profession, had something done every year. In a way it was surprising she had waited so long; she supposed she must have been a little proud. But Jorge had been so taken with the idea, and then later, so pleased with the results. She could have paid for it herself but he would not have it and the money made no difference to him. 'Now I own part of you,' he had joked afterwards.

Her breasts floated just under the surface. She touched them and then held them with her hands, as if they were not part of her own body. She did not think they were absurd, as she had overheard one of the other actresses saying. She agreed with Jorge; they were beautiful. She took a deep breath and slid down into the bath, pulling her head underwater. She closed her eyes and felt warmed through.

There was someone standing in the bathroom doorway. For a moment she thought, Jorge. But it was not Jorge. Of course it was not. It was the maid, whose name she could not now remember.

'I'm very sorry, Mrs Echegary. I knocked for a long time.' She hesitated. 'Are you all right?' She looked at the bottle she was holding, the champagne Luisa had ordered and forgotten about. 'I'll leave it on the bar.'

'Don't be silly,' said Luisa, sitting up in the bath. 'What is your name?' She was sober enough to notice that she was slurring her words.

'Mariana.'

'Yes. Don't be silly, Mariana. Open the bottle. I need you to fill up my glass.'

The maid hesitated and then popped the champagne cork and walked across the room.

'If you don't look at what you're doing you'll spill it,' said Luisa, smiling. 'Now pour yourself a glass. There's another one in the other room.'

'I can't, Mrs Echegary. I'm working.'

'Luisa. Please call me Luisa. This is working. I am a good customer. You can have a drink with me. Otherwise,' she said lightly, 'I will complain about you.'

The maid got the glass from the bedroom. She sat on the edge of a chair by the sink and held the champagne rigidly in front of her.

'How old are you, Mariana?'

'I'm nineteen.'

'How old do you think I am?'

The maid looked past Luisa at the mottled glass of the bathroom window. 'I don't know, Mrs Echegary.'

Luisa waved her hand in the air. 'It doesn't matter. You have a very nice figure, Mariana.'

'Thank you.'

'Jorge would admire you. He would like your body. It is a pity they make you wear that uniform.'

The maid stood up.

'I have to go. The manager –'

'Let him wait,' said Luisa, with a sharpness she had not intended.

She lay back in the bath, not speaking, and for several minutes she watched the champagne bubbles race up the side of the glass and pop at the surface.

Then, still holding the glass in her left hand, she gripped the side of the bath with her right and began to pull herself to her feet. The water ran off her body in streams and again she felt the rawness of her skin. She felt terribly heavy but did not stop. She pushed away the hair that was plastered across her eyes and stood up as straight as she could manage. She held her arms out wide.

'This is what Jorge likes,' she said. 'This is why he comes here.'

She felt dizzy. She staggered forward and the champagne slopped out of her glass into the water below. The maid stepped closer but Luisa held onto the window ledge and steadied herself. She turned to the maid.

'We should have a toast. What should we have a toast to, Mariana?'

'I don't know, Mrs Echegary,' said the maid, still poised halfway across the room. 'To you?'

Luisa laughed. 'Yes, of course. To me.' She let go of the window ledge. She raised the glass in front of her and tilted it forward, knocking it against an imaginary other.

'To me, then,' she said.

Perhaps the light shed by the chandelier was less kind than the sunlight had been but, as she got dressed, it seemed to Luisa that in the months she had been coming here the room had become perceptibly shabbier. They had chosen the hotel because it was not ostentatious but now she noticed the thinness of the carpets and their old-fashioned floral pattern, the shiny vulgarity of the furnishings, the cheapness of the champagne flutes. There was a yellow-brown tobacco stain on the ceiling above the bed.

She took her time dressing, drying her hair and putting on make-up, and when she finally left the room she felt more hung-over than drunk. In the lobby she paid the bill and cancelled the reservations for the following week. She asked the manager to light one of her cigarillos and he gave her his card. Outside it was dark, not even dusky. The valet had disappeared so she walked across the car park to her car. She tried the driver's door before remembering it was broken. She went round to the passenger's side, climbed over the gearstick, and started the car.

You Must Change Your Life

LAURIE WAS STANDING AT THE KITCHEN WINDOW, LOOKING into the garden – daydreaming, his wife would have said – when the first object flew over the back fence. Initially, he could not tell what it was. It appeared as a dark streak in front of his eyes. He was startled and slopped the tea he was drinking onto the tiled floor. The object landed in the middle of the lawn and he went out to have a look. It was a shoe – a brown leather brogue, the left one of the pair, perhaps a size eleven or twelve, expensive-looking but now battered. He knelt over the shoe, obscurely reluctant to touch it, as if it were some coiled animal that might react unpredictably. Then he picked it up and stood for a moment, wondering what he should do. He had a brief image of a tall, rumpled man limping up to the front door to claim it, apologising for the trouble. Laurie carried the shoe round to the side of the house, placed it in a box in the garage and went back inside. By the time his wife and daughter arrived home, he had forgotten all about the incident. Even if he had not, he might not have thought it worth mentioning.

Then, two days later, there was something else. This time he did not see the object arrive. He had been out for a walk and when he came back, around lunchtime, it was there, lying in approximately the same place as the shoe – a child's teddy bear, a short trail of thread where one of its eyes had been.

Laurie looked towards the bottom of the garden, the direction from which the shoe had arrived and – he could only assume – the bear as well. Beyond the fence was a row of tall conifers and, just visible behind them, a large modern building, some kind of home or institution for the mentally ill. Laurie had been past it many times. From the front it was an innocuous-looking place, all red brick and glass, with a car park off to one side, not unlike a school or a library. He did not know exactly who lived there or what their problems were, but he sometimes saw them – listless, agitated individuals – walking around the neighbourhood.

Laurie walked to the bottom of the garden, holding the bear under his arm.

'Hello,' he called out tentatively, alert to his own ridiculousness. No reply.

'Hello,' he said again.

That evening, as he was giving his daughter Jess her dinner, it occurred to him to tell her about the shoe and about the bear. Since he had given up his job he often felt he had too little to say to her about his day, that it was hard to account for himself. In its mystery and strangeness, this had the qualities of something that would intrigue her. He would describe himself creeping towards the fence and then calling out, embroidering the incident with little details that would make her laugh. But this would also mean sharing it with Marianne, his wife.

There were two ways the conversation might go. Marianne might see it as further evidence of how he spent his days: staring out of the window, preoccupying himself with things that were not important, waiting for something to happen. She might even imply that it was a figment of his understimulated imagination, that he had made more of it than it really was – and there was no denying the fact that he had been there at the window the precise moment the shoe had come over, almost as if he had conjured it up himself. Alternatively – and this was no more enticing – she might take it seriously. She would point out the danger to both her and Jess of objects being thrown into the garden without warning, and it would be hard to argue with this. She might insist that he go round to the home and investigate. Either way, it would rebound on him.

When Jess had just turned two, there had nearly been a terrible accident. Laurie was bathing her, as he did most nights, and left the room for what – he swore later – could only have been a few seconds. When he got back Jess's head was underwater and she was struggling. In the event she was shocked rather than hurt, but there was an awful row. 'You're a fool,' Marianne shouted at Laurie. 'Something distracted me,' he said later, when things had calmed down, though he could not say what.

It was also around this time that Laurie had suddenly decided to give up his job in a university. It was not the job itself – it could be boring or stressful at times but he did not especially dislike it. No, the idea had come to him, so it seemed, out of nowhere. One morning a woman on the street had handed him a gaudily printed leaflet emblazoned with the words *You Must Change Your Life*. Later, he could not remember what was in the leaflet, or if he had even read it – some evangelical or cultish nonsense, no doubt – but over the next few days and weeks the phrase kept coming back to him with the strength of an order, or a necessity.

He remembered the conversation with Marianne clearly.

She had regarded him sceptically for several seconds, as if intent on discovering from his expression whether this was some kind of joke.

'It's hardly the time, Laurie. There's the mortgage, child-care . . .'

She was right, of course, but Marianne was doing well in her work. As a lawyer she earned nearly twice what Laurie did. They would get by.

'I know, I know,' he said. 'I just have the sense that this is something important I need to do.'

'But what,' said Marianne, 'what do you need to do?'

He had a vague notion of the things he might do – anything was possible! – but this, to Laurie, seemed like missing the point. Much stronger than this, than any fixed idea of how he might spend his time, was the radical nature of the instruction, and it was only this that had caught in his mind – *You Must Change Your Life* – so bright and emphatic that it cast everything beyond it into shadow.

Over the next month many more objects came over the fence. There was no pattern – three things would arrive during one afternoon and then nothing for several days. There were bits of clothing – a woolly hat, a shirt, a scarf, the other brogue – as well as a rucksack, a cushion, a cardboard box and an old paperback book. Throughout the day Laurie kept a wary eye on the garden, and each time he spotted something on the lawn, or, occasionally, caught in the branches of the conifers that hung over the fence, he went out and removed it to the box in the garage.

When he had given up work, Laurie had recognised the importance of keeping to a routine, of being purposeful – after all, it was not laziness that motivated his decision.

To that end he got up early to spend time with Jess. At half past eight Marianne took her to nursery and then went on to her work. Once they had left the house Laurie read each section of the newspaper from front to back before going out for a walk. After lunch, he went out again, often for a swim. He carried around with him a notebook in which he wrote down things as they occurred to him, or drew quick and – he did not deceive himself – rather crude sketches. He drew diagrams too, complex networks of boxes and arrows that suggested how all these different thoughts and ideas might be linked together. He had it in mind that this would form the beginning of whatever it was he was going to do. It was vague, he knew, but Laurie was confident that from this structure, these good intentions, something meaningful would gradually emerge.

However, the appearance of these objects in the garden became a distraction. When he was reading or walking or writing in his book, he often found himself wondering whether anything new had arrived. He sometimes stood at the kitchen window, in the pose he had been in when the shoe had appeared, anticipating what would come next.

Laurie asked himself what, if anything, it meant. One or two objects were not significant – a prank, someone's passing whim, an accident even – but now he could not avoid the idea that there was some intention to it, a message, a statement, even a cry for help. He felt somehow that he was being appealed to, called upon to act. Each time something new arrived, he contemplated going round to the home, imagined himself climbing the steps to the front door and handing everything over to a member of staff, but each time he went out into the garden, picked up the object, placed it in the box in the garage and went back inside.

But the box was filling up. At some point Marianne would notice and he would have to explain what had been going on. It was awkward. It would be hard now to tell the truth and justify why he had not mentioned it before. At best, he would appear perverse, at a time when his judgement was already regarded as faulty. It had been strange and futile to conceal it in the first place and now, as a result of the subterfuge he was engaged in, the arrival of each new thing had become freighted with a budding anxiety. Still Laurie did not take the box back. He had begun, irrationally he knew, to feel that these objects were the manifestation of something indefinably volatile or malign beyond the fence.

Then, one Saturday morning when Marianne was out and he was in the garden with Jess, a black leather belt with a heavy buckle landed only a few feet from where she was playing, and Laurie knew he could not put it off any longer.

He had not imagined that he would meet the person responsible. On Monday morning, as he walked the ten-minute route round to the home, he imagined that he would simply stand at the entrance and explain the situation to a member of staff, say that he did not care who had been throwing these things over the fence, only that it stopped, hand over the box and be on his way – and in this light he could not see why he had put off coming round for so long. But when Laurie stepped through the front door – it was heavy and as it opened he felt a rush of warm, slightly stale air on his face – and described it all to the young man who came out to meet him, the man nodded thoughtfully and waved him in.

He was left sitting in a reception area. There were flowers

on the table and pictures on the wall, institutional like a doctor's waiting room, but somehow brighter and more cheerful than he had expected. Despite this, he felt a throb of the anxiety he had come to associate with the whole business.

'This is Jonathan,' said the man who had met him at the door. Another man had followed him into the room, but remained just inside the doorway, his face and body turned away.

'Hello, Jonathan,' said Laurie, 'I'm Laurie.'

Laurie did not recognise him. He was not one of the afflicted individuals he had seen walking around the neighbourhood, although he caught immediately the same odd air of listlessness and agitation. He was heavily built and tall, quite big enough to be the owner of the brogues, but uncomfortable in his bigness, a little stooped, unequal to his physical presence. He was wearing suit trousers that were too small for him, sandals and a T-shirt advertising Coors beer, a look that Laurie saw would, in other circumstances, have been rather comic.

Laurie put out his hand and then, when Jonathan did not move, let it drop to his side. There was a silence, and Laurie wondered whether, if he had still been working and not spending so much time in his own company, he would have known what to say or do. Perhaps he would have better handled a situation like this.

'Laurie has brought your things back. You've been throwing them into his garden.'

At this, Jonathan turned and took a step into the room. Laurie saw that he was much older than he had at first seemed. It was hard to know – his eyes and the pattern of lines on his face suggested some depth or intensity of experience rather than simply age. The way he had been standing had concealed the left side of his body but Laurie could now also see that his arm was heavily bandaged, from the elbow to the wrist, and that he held it gingerly against his chest.

Laurie reached into the box and held up the shoes. 'Thanks for these but they're not my size.' He thought to put him at ease, to turn it all into an innocent joke between them – but Jonathan retreated to the doorway with a look of alarm.

Laurie had come in order to complain but now he felt the necessity of saying something hopeful or consoling, something to absolve Jonathan of any guilt or embarrassment he might feel, but he could not think what. He looked around the room. At the far end someone sat behind a glass screen, writing in a folder. He wanted to say, 'I'm sorry that you're here at all, I'm sorry for your problems, whatever they are,' but knew that this was useless as well as absurd. He wondered if he should ask about his arm but quickly dismissed it. He was at a loss.

There was a sudden crackle of sound and a voice came over a speaker system. It said something brief and unintelligible before there was another crackle of noise and then silence.

'My daughter,' said Laurie, wishing immediately that he had not mentioned Jess, 'my daughter plays in the garden. She might have been hurt.' Silence again. 'You can keep the box,' he said helplessly.

'Don't worry,' said the man who had let him in, 'just leave everything here. We'll have a word. It won't happen again.'

Jonathan had already disappeared out of the door.

* * *

On the way home Laurie felt thoroughly unburdened, elated even. How had it gone? It was impossible to say, but at least it had been done, duty discharged. Once you faced these things, he reflected, they lost their power to affect you. He had no explanation for what had been happening but he decided now that there was no explanation – it meant nothing.

Over the next few days, no new items arrived and things had even come out, more or less, with Marianne, in a way that reflected positively on Laurie. Jess had said something to her about the belt that had been thrown into the garden. When Marianne brought it up with Laurie he explained that he had been round to the home and dealt with it.

'Curious sort of place,' he said. 'You wonder what goes on there.'

Marianne raised her eyebrows. Laurie did not mention the other items and this did not seem like a significant deception.

However, a week later, as he was getting breakfast for Jess, he noticed something in the garden. It was the shoe – lying in approximately the same place on the lawn as before. He wondered how long it had been there. The following day, as he was standing at the kitchen window, the bear came over the fence.

'It won't happen again,' the man had said. Laurie had been round to the home, he had been reasonable and yet now this. In the coming days and weeks, as the objects continued to arrive, he found himself going over the original encounter – brief and unremarkable as it had seemed to be – recalling each detail and everything that was said. It was an odd sensation but he was no longer sure if it was really as he had experienced it. There was something, something beyond the obvious, an undertow, that in his nervousness or complacency he had missed. He had misread the situation, its significance, and this was the result. The relief he had felt was entirely false.

Laurie thought often of Jonathan. He wondered what, at any given time, he was doing. He imagined him walking the corridors of the home or alone in his room, his bandaged arm held against his chest. He recalled details that he had not seemed to notice at the time – a mole on Jonathan's cheek, the porthole-like windows and thick, wired glass in all the doors. Several times when Laurie was out he spotted him, his distinctive size and way of carrying himself. On each occasion he had been about to go up to him, in the park or at a bus stop, when the person would turn and show themselves to be someone else, not even a likeness. At these times Laurie felt as if his life was perpetually shadowed by Jonathan's unknowable days.

It came to Laurie one afternoon as he sat in the park, with his notebook balanced on his knee and the hours stretching in front of him, that he was no closer now, months on, to knowing what he was doing. He had barely written in the book for several weeks, and when he had it was to briefly record where he had been and what he had done. It was clear – nothing had announced itself and only a stubborn optimism had sustained the project this far. All he really had was a title – *You Must Change Your Life* – and even this lacked the clarity and force it had once seemed to have. The rest – the rest was just jottings, entirely trivial and self-indulgent. When he looked at his diagrams they were hard to make out, like scribbles in code or a different language altogether, with no clue as to what it was they were supposed to describe or illuminate. What on earth, he asked himself, had he imagined he was doing? He was only thankful that he had not confided it, to Marianne or anyone else.

Six weeks later, in July, Laurie returned to work. By luck his old job had come up again and they were happy to have him back. He could not deny that it was good to be working again. He took pleasure in the small things, the little routines. Very quickly, the previous eight months became hazy in his mind, as if it were in the distant past, or even a part of someone else's life that he had only been told about. Marianne began to refer it as 'Laurie's existential crisis' or 'Laurie's grey period', and her sarcasm also helped to put it at a comfortable remove. When he did think about it, it did not seem so dramatic or so strange a thing to have done, just some kind of necessary readjustment, a chance to get things in perspective. The objects continued to arrive from time to time but he was able to put it out of his mind. The sense of ticking dread that he had felt when he was at home had all but gone. The box was nearly full again. In time, he thought, he would return it to the home.

Every Saturday, Laurie took Jess swimming and it was on one of these trips, after he had been back working for several weeks, that he saw Jonathan again. They had changed into their things and Jess joined her class in the children's pool. Laurie climbed down into the main pool and began to swim lengths. These swims were one of the few links he felt between life now and during the 'grey period'. It was then that he had begun to swim regularly and it seemed to have perhaps been the only useful legacy of that time. It relaxed him. He liked to lose himself in the distortion of everything – the mottled light across the surface of the water, the shifting patterns of the pool markings below, the rush of noise each time his head came out of the water and sudden muting as it went in again. As he found his rhythm, the action and exertion of his body seemed to absorb everything into it, the yellowy glare of the lights, the chlorine smell, the white noise of shrieking and whistles being blown. If you got it right, Laurie thought, even in this unlikely place, you could manage a kind of meditativeness, a temporary peace. Each time he approached the smaller pool he could spot Jess among the other children by raising his head higher out of the water, the ribbon tying back her hair and the sky blue of her armbands. He had done six lengths and could do another twenty before her class had finished.

He was not sure at first that it was Jonathan. Laurie had mistaken him often enough before to doubt himself. He was part of a group that were standing in the shallow end, in a roped-off part of the pool. They made a strange sight, ten or so of them – dazed by their surroundings, apparently nervous of the water, their bodies pale and neglected. A woman in shorts and flip-flops stood above them on the edge of the pool, shouting to make herself heard over the din and demonstrating a stroke with her hands. Laurie checked for Jess, turned and pushed off for another length.

As he came back again he saw clearly that it was Jonathan. He had detached himself slightly from the group and was standing against the rope, blinking up at the lights. The water barely came up to his waist and he had wrapped his arms tightly around his body, to keep himself warm or perhaps in some other protective gesture. On one arm, the one that had been bandaged, there was a long scar, healed but still raw against his white skin. Unclothed, he seemed even larger and more out of place in his own body than when Laurie had seen him at the home. A sharp pang of pity went through him. As he swam towards the end and then turned and pushed off, Laurie was close enough to reach out and touch the scar.

Halfway through his length, it occurred to Laurie that he had not checked for Jess on his last approach. He had been preoccupied with Jonathan. As he continued to make his way towards the far end of the pool the thought gathered urgency – he could not dismiss it. He had not checked for Jess – the endless reflex of checking, the unconscious habit of a thousand times a day had somehow let him down – and it would be nearly a minute before he would be back at the other end. By which time anything – he did not know what – might have happened to her.

The thought was absurd, he knew. Laurie concentrated on his stroke and his breathing, keeping them strong and even. He told himself that even if there were something wrong then a consistent stroke would bring him to her more quickly. He was nearly at the far end and he could get out and look or walk back to reassure himself. But this would be giving in to the anxiety – and it suddenly seemed to him that he must keep on swimming as he was, that this was imperative in what was to happen, that he must go on, as if he could control the situation by his attitude to it. He would swim strongly and evenly and calmly and when he reached the other end he would see Jess and all would be well.

It was no good. He turned underwater and pushed off the side. The opposite end of the pool was a blur in the far distance and approaching with dreamlike slowness.

Laurie felt his heartbeat quicken, his breaths come shorter and shallower, and he knew he was moving more slowly, not faster, through the water. Each time he raised his head to take a breath the noise of the pool seemed to have risen in pitch and intensity. Where before the shrieking and abrupt whistles of the guards had been absorbed into his stroke, part of the force that moved his body through the water, now there was something profoundly oppressive to them. The roar in his ears seemed like that of a gathering emergency, a calamity – or, alternatively, designed to drown out and distract from the disaster he felt certain was unfolding.

He was halfway back now, and he could see clearly the shallow end of the pool. Jonathan was not where he had been, against the ropes, as Laurie had already known he would not be. The group from the home were still there, looking vaguely up at their instructor, but he could not make out Jonathan among them. He scanned the sides of the pool but there was no sign. As he came up again for a breath, Laurie looked for Jess, although he knew there was no view of the children's pool from this distance. His arms were weary, leaden. He knew that he was not getting enough oxygen into his body. It seemed that he was barely moving forward, that his flailing stroke was futile against the weight and resistance of the water. As he looked ahead there was a horrible glare all around him, as if everything was emitting the same sharp white light.

Then he was there at the other end. Exhausted, Laurie dragged himself out of the water and on to the side. Immediately, he saw Jess, just ahead of him in the children's pool. Supported by one of the instructors, she was splashing her way from one end to the other. Her expression was fixed in a fury of concentration, her arms and legs pounding the water, and as she reached the end she grabbed for the side and shouted out in delight.

Laurie took two short steps and sat down against the wall. For several minutes he watched as Jess swam back and forth across the pool, somehow moved by the fact that she did not know he was there or watching. There was no sign of Jonathan. He had gone again. Then, when he had caught his breath, and the strength had returned to his legs and arms, Laurie stood up and called to her.

San Francisco

WE HAVE BEEN IN THE CITY FOR THREE WEEKS. THERE ARE rumours that the political situation in the country is deteriorating. I ask you, once again, to change the channel on the television. You say nothing and I ask again and you say, why?

I say, to watch the news, I want to see about the political situation.

You say, why do you care? They don't report it anyway.

You are right, of course, and I say nothing.

You will not leave our room. You say the altitude makes you sick. You say that the thin air makes you so sick you have to lie on the bed all day and smoke cigarettes and watch TV. You say you know what's out there anyway, there are too many hills to climb. It reminds you of San Francisco.

I am surprised. I say, have you ever been to San Francisco?

You say, I haven't.

I say, how can it remind you of San Francisco if you haven't ever been to San Francisco?

I haven't been there, you say, but I know what it looks like. You point out the window. That's what it looks like, you say.

You say you are not leaving this room until Ramiro comes and then you are leaving this room.

When is Ramiro coming? I say.

Soon, you say, but you always say that.

I say, I have been to San Francisco. It doesn't remind me of San Francisco.

We met a month ago in the south of the country. You told me I had beautiful arms. I believe you only said it because it is something someone once said to you and you liked it.

You had beautiful arms and astonishing eyes, and seemed to me very exotic. It was hard to know what was in it for you but I was not foolish enough to ask.

You told me you liked the way our skin looked together, yours dark and mine pale, like different kinds of corn, you said. Now that I have been in the sun for longer the contrast is not so great but you have not remarked upon it.

You are not from this country but you are from the same continent and speak the same language. You said you loved your country with its great rivers and endless skies and you wished you could show it to me. You said you loved your continent and were proud of it, despite its troubles. You said the whole continent was your country and all its people your people.

I said I wanted to learn your language and you called me your gringo burro and said you would teach me and we made love.

The bank is cool and quiet. The clerk holds my last traveller's cheque up to the light. He looks at me over his spectacles and asks me to sign it. He files it away and opens the till. I ask him if he thinks the political situation in the country is very bad.

Tens or twenties, he says.

Excuse me? I say, in his language.

The money, tens or twenties?

Tens, I say, it's easier. He does not smile.

On the way back to the hotel I suddenly see what you mean about San Francisco, the hills, the cars, the wires that hang like vines across the street.

When I get back to the room you say, Ramiro phoned.

I say, he did? You are lying on the bed, watching the soap opera. I find it hard to believe you have moved to speak to someone on the phone.

You say, yes, he did.

So are we leaving? I say.

You say, not yet, there has been a delay.

Again, I say. I say, what is the delay?

You say, Ramiro says everything is fine. He says we should relax and enjoy his country.

I do not tell you how the city reminded me of San Francisco.

We had been in the city for one day when you said, the best thing about this town is that cigarettes last forever.

You had bought cocaine, from Ramiro, and we were in our room, doing it. You timed how long it took you to smoke a cigarette. You estimated that it was 50 per cent longer than normal. That's value for money, you said.

You said, the cigarette companies can't have realised otherwise they would have put something in them to make them burn faster. You said it felt good to be getting one over on the cigarette companies and you would smoke as many as you could before they cottoned on.

Or you die, I said.

Or that, you said.

You did more cocaine and so did I and I said that I had

an idea for Smokers Holidays to the city. Come to Beautiful ——— , where cigarettes last twice as long.

You were standing on the bed. This is what it's like smoking on the moon, you said. You were waving your cigarette in your hand, getting carried away. You said, imagine what it would be like to smoke a cigarette on the moon.

You took a drag on your cigarette. You looked at it and you laughed. I said, the worst thing about this town is that cigarettes sometimes go out.

There are always people in the hotel reception. They watch TV. It is always the same soap opera that is on, the same one that you watch. I do not understand what the actors are saying but I am beginning to recognise the characters. The people in reception don't speak much. I try to ask them about the political situation and they snigger at my attempts. Once, when I sneezed, they laughed hysterically. They held their heads and rocked in their chairs. They couldn't stop.

I say to you, why don't the people in reception like me?

You laugh and say, because you are gringo burro.

Of course, I say, I am the gringo donkey. But why don't they like me?

You say, because you always ask them about the political situation.

In the time we have been in the hotel many other tourists have come and gone. We have met a number of them. One man, a Russian, we met before in the south of the country. He was always eating fruit. You could not stand him. When we arrived in the hotel he was there, in reception.

He didn't say, hello, he said, I'm in love. His hands ran

with the juice of a papaya. It was smeared in his goatee beard. He said, isn't this town something? I'm in love, this town is really something.

We met him a month ago. Since we have known him he has been in love with many different women. His idea of love was to see someone he would like to sleep with. He had been in love with you too, once.

Another man at the hotel had an accent it was hard to place. It had streaks of everywhere in it. He asked me if I played chess and I said, yes, a little. We played in the court-yard.

He said the people in the room next to him made a lot of noise at night, he thought they might be criminals of some kind. He had no problem with fornicators, he said, as long as he didn't have to listen to them. He said, I guess you can't choose your neighbours, huh? He said, you get what you're given, right?

He did not concentrate on the game. He wanted to talk. He had been travelling for years and had complaints about everywhere he'd been. In this country he didn't like the small bananas that tasted like apples. He said, if I buy a banana, I want it to taste like a banana, right?

I moved my queen. Check, I said.

He looked at the board. It's checkmate, he said, in his funny everywhere accent.

Is it? I said. I didn't realise.

He said, don't you know how to play? It's checkmate. Don't you know how to play?

Ramiro knows everyone in the city. He knows the people in reception. This is one of the things that makes me nervous.

You met him in reception the day we arrived and he

invited us to a bar he had just opened. We were new in town so we went to the bar in the evening. It wasn't much of a place. There was no one else there and he made a great fuss of us. He gave us drinks and taught us dice games that only local people knew. The games were not very good but the drinks were strong and everyone had a good time.

We surprised ourselves by telling Ramiro about our love affair. We were embarrassed when we told him we had only known each other for a month but he said it was unimportant and that love was love, if it were one day or fifty years. He said he believed in love and it made him feel good to hear about other people's.

We told him about our plan to build a bar and some cottages at a place that you knew on the coast of your country that was wild and unspoiled. You had uncles that could help us with the building and the business side. The only problem, we said, was that we would need money, but we believed in it and everything else would take care of itself.

Ramiro was delighted with us. He said we were beautiful lovers and that when we married he would expect to be invited and he would come. Then he was sad. He said that he had been married. It was when he was in the air force. He was married and he had a child but they were killed in circumstances that he couldn't bring himself to tell us about. Then he stopped being sad and poured more drinks. He said he had friends all over the country and we must tell him whatever we needed and he would help us.

That is when you asked him if he knew where we could

buy some cocaine. He said, of course, for two lovers such as yourselves it will be no problem.

I lie on the bed. I lie on the bed and try to concentrate on the soap opera. There is a lot of dark wood in the houses and it looks like the 1970s. Nothing ever happens outside. I do not understand what the people are saying but it is not hard to follow the story. The characters are passionate people with quivering lips. There are many tense pauses and the storylines are always about betrayal. The actors have lighter skin than the people on the street in the city. They do not seem to suffer from altitude sickness.

Are you feeling any better? I ask you.

No, you say, no better.

I say, the altitude did not affect you at first.

Not at first, no, do you think I am lying?

No, I say, I don't think you're lying.

A cigarette lasts 50 per cent longer than normal, you say. That's how much less oxygen there is. That's how much less air I am getting. No wonder I feel bad.

I say, I'm not sure that follows.

Gringo burro, you say.

I say, if Ramiro does not come soon we will have no money left.

I no longer talk to you about the political situation.

What I know I know from hearing bits of conversation around the city. On street corners and in shops I hear the words for soldiers and rebels and beatings and disappearances. I know the words for these things, the sound of them is satisfying, but I do not know the little words that surround them and give them meaning. I try to talk to people when I hear them say these words but I cannot make myself understood. They look blank and ask, in my language, do I like their country, and I say, yes, it's very beautiful.

When you are on the toilet or in the shower I switch the TV over to the news. There are reports of strange accidents and natural disasters that do not quite add up. Once, very early in the morning, I went out for a walk. I saw convoys of trucks carrying troops leaving the city, heading south.

The man with the voice from everywhere comes to our door. He is holding the chessboard and wants to play. He is trying to get a good look into the room. I look over at you, lying on the bed, and I say, yes, I'll play.

He says, over my shoulder, talking to you, he says, you can play the winner.

I close the door. She's sick, I say. Anyway, she doesn't play.

We sit down in the courtyard and set up the game.

He says, so she's sick, huh? I nod.

Everyone gets sick, he says. That's the way life goes, right?

The Russian walks out of reception and into the courtyard. He has a mango in each hand. He pulls up a chair and starts to cut into the fruit. I'm in love, he says.

The man with the voice makes mistakes. I take his queen. He makes a face like it was a great move.

He says, I concede, right? Sometimes you just have to concede. You want another game? he says. I shake my head and he picks up the board. He goes back into his room, the one next to mine and yours. The table is covered in slime from the mangoes.

I'm in love, says the Russian.

We stopped going to Ramiro's bar two weeks ago. He said it was better that way. Since then you have been sick and have had to lie on the bed smoking cigarettes and watching TV. Ramiro calls on the phone, sometimes, and speaks to you. I do not understand the conversations. You talk very fast and I wonder if it is deliberate. After you put the phone down you light a cigarette and I say, well?

You say, everything is fine. There has been a delay.

You do not look at me, you talk to the TV.

I say, how long?

A couple of days, you say. You say, everything is fine, Ramiro says hello.

Last week I suggested we leave the city for a few days. I said we could go to another town, down towards the jungle. It would be a change and you might not feel so sick, I said.

Changes in altitude do terrible things to my ears, you said. We would only have to come back, you said. You said, Ramiro says it could be any time, we should be ready to leave. This is your best argument and it is not a very good one.

Now we have a hotel bill that we cannot pay. Now we have no money and could not leave even if you wanted to.

You refuse to teach me your language. You say I only want to understand so that I can ask about the political situation. I ask you what is wrong with that and you shrug and say, if you really wanted to learn you would watch the soap opera, it is really very good.

You are not from this country but you are from the same continent and speak the same language. You are sneering about the people here. You say they have no culture. You say that even the soap opera is filmed in your country and I am surprised because you have never thought to mention it before.

I have become wary of Ramiro's promises. I have become wary of his promises and I try to tell you this but it makes you angry as I knew it would.

He is trying to help us, you say. He believes in us and he is trying to help us.

I say, but now the political situation is deteriorating. We do not know who works for the authorities.

You say, you did not care about the political situation at first.

I say, you were not sick at first.

You say, you are obsessed with the political situation.

Do you want to fuck Ramiro? I say.

You say, you think everyone is working for the authorities.

I say, are you fucking Ramiro?

The man with the voice from everywhere and I play chess in the courtyard. The Russian is sitting with us. He is using a long knife to dissect a pineapple but he does not speak. The man with the voice does not like how they weigh your food in restaurants and you pay accordingly. He says, why don't I like it? I have my own way, right? Everybody has their own way, he says.

Four men are dressed in green and are talking to the people in reception. They are carrying guns and are either soldiers or police.

The man from everywhere moves his queen and says, it's not the money. I have money in the bank. You know what I'm saying, I don't have to worry.

The men in green come over to where we are sitting, the Russian, the man from everywhere and me. They say something to the Russian then pull him up by his shoulders. They walk him out towards reception. The Russian hides the pineapple behind his back.

The man from everywhere shrugs his shoulders. He knocks over his king and says, I concede, right? You want another game?

I have many friends, Ramiro had said.

I have been thinking about your plan, he said, and I want to help you. I want to help you because I like you, because you are lovers, and I was a lover once.

We were drunk and had not slept for days and still it did not seem like a good idea.

Trust me, you said.

I don't know, I said. For one thing, there is the political situation to think of.

There is always that, you said, but trust me.

I don't know, I said.

You held out your beautiful arms and touched me. You said, perhaps you were not serious about our plan? You smiled and fixed me with your astonishing eyes. You said, perhaps you were not serious about the bar and the cottages and the wild unspoiled coast? You lay down next to me, your skin still dark against mine.

You said, quietly, perhaps you were not serious when you said you loved me?

* * *

Ramiro phones and says everything is ready. You tell me that this is what he says. You tell me that you are too sick to go. You say that you have already told Ramiro that I will be going alone.

Someone comes to the hotel to pick me up. I had been expecting Ramiro. In the courtyard the Russian and the man from everywhere are sharing a bunch of bananas, the small kind that taste like apples. They do not notice me. In reception there are three people watching TV. The soap opera is on.

We drive up, out of the city. I talk to the man who is not Ramiro but we cannot understand each other. I can remember some of the words you taught me but not how to put them together. We drive up and I can taste the thinness of the air and I think it is as well that you have not come, it would only have made you sick.

After two hours the driver stops the car. He shakes my hand and waits for me to open the door and get out. He shouts something out of the window as he pulls away. It sounds familiar but I do not catch it. I watch the clouds of dust that blow up behind the car for a long time after it has disappeared from view, thinking about what it is he might have said.

There is nothing but bare mountains and stones. I think that this is what the moon must look like. The sun is bright but I am shivering with the cold. Nothing moves in the air, it is empty, pressed up against the sky. I try to light a cigarette but cannot get a flame. I think of you, lying on our bed. I wonder what is happening in the soap opera, if you are even watching it.

From a long way off I see clouds of dust and, behind them, a truck approaching.

I feel dizzy, a little sick. I try to light a cigarette but it is hopeless. It is not until the truck is nearly upon me that the thin air lets me hear the sound it makes.

Border

HAMILTON IS TALKING ABOUT ALL THE THINGS HE WILL HAVE when he gets across the border. He will have a red car, long and thin and low to the ground, with a leather interior (he says he already knows what the leather will smell like). He will have a television with a screen like this, he says, and stretches his arms out wide, like someone pinned to a cross. He will have a house with more rooms than he has a use for and a kitchen with a fridge that dispenses chilled water and crushed ice at the push of a button. Hamilton smiles, showing his teeth. He will get his teeth fixed, he says, and wear tailored suits and aftershave from a tiny bottle.

All of us in the hotel have heard this before. We have all seen the collage of pictures stuck to the wall above Hamilton's bed, pictures he has cut carefully from the magazines provided by the owner of the hotel. We could all add to the list of things he will have when he gets across the border: a girl with blonde hair and a wide, white smile to sit beside him in his long low car; a garden with a swimming pool; Cuban cigars.

Hamilton is not his real name. It is the name of a character in a television show from across the border. At first some of the other people in the hotel mocked him. They called him the names of famous people, movie stars or revolutionaries, or made up insulting nicknames. When he did not respond they would call him by his real name. Then his head would come up and he would make a great show of looking around. 'Who are you talking to?' he would say. 'Is there a new guest in the hotel? Won't someone introduce us?' Soon they tired of their teasing and now no one remembers what he is really called. Sometimes they argue about it but no one is sure. Perhaps the hotel owner knows, but he does not say.

The hotel is not far from the border. This is one of the reasons that the rooms are always full. Also, the hotel is three storeys high and there are views from the roof. The hotel owner has provided plastic chairs up there and calls it 'the roof garden'. To the east, the west and the south you can see a long way, for miles, to where the names of political candidates and their parties are painted in giant white letters across the cracked hills. We do not look that way. The chairs are pulled up to the side that faces north towards the border. You can look towards the border although you cannot see clearly to the other side. The town crowds in on our view. There are billboards, buildings sprouting with poles and waiting for another floor to be added, a spider's web of aerials, spires and cranes. You cannot see much, but it is enough. Looking across the street in front of the hotel there is a gap between two government buildings. Through the gap and past the dome of a church, an advertisement for a soft drink stands on posts on the top of a factory. Between the top of the factory and the brash colours of the advertisement is a window of blue sky. I think this sky must be on the other side. I watch it, day by day, and tell myself that it is. I can see it better if I squint.

The hotel owner calls us his guests. In the mornings he joins us on the roof. 'Why do I bother to purchase chairs for my guests to sit on?' he says, though no one has asked him why. 'Because it is good business. Because I am selling a dream. And it is good business to let people see what they are buying.' He laughs. It is for the same reason that he provides the magazines.

Sometimes he talks about life across the border. He encourages Hamilton's fantasies. 'Everything is different over there,' he says. He sniffs the air. 'Even the air is different across the border. Cleaner, cooler.' We do not believe much of what he says but that does not mean we do not listen. Occasionally someone will tire of his talk and ask him why, if life across the border is so good, he is here and not there. He enjoys answering this question. 'Because my guests are here,' he says, 'and business is business.'

The guests sit up on the roof in the morning, before it gets too hot and before the dust begins to sweep in from the east. We are there in the evening too, when the heat and the dust have passed. There is little talk, except for Hamilton. Some play cards, or smoke. Most of us sit in the plastic chairs and look for ways through the buildings and aerials, the billboards and spires, north towards the border.

Often, when he comes to my room at night, the hotel owner tells me that I will do well across the border. His hair is long and lank, his face pitted like the land to the east. More hair erupts from his ears and nostrils. His teeth, like everyone's, are bad. He wears flip-flops, grubby white shorts and a torn flannel shirt. And yet his hands, when he places them on my leg, as he always does, are soft, delicate, feminine even. The fingernails are immaculately clean, perfectly trimmed and polished. He begins nervously, like a too excited child, like a man used to being denied. He traces his finger slowly, softly along the peaks and troughs of my spine. He touches my breasts. He tries to caress. Then he pulls me from the bed and turns me against the wall. He holds my hair from behind and when he tells me I will do well across the border, that there are 'opportunities' for a girl like me, I think of the window of sky I can see from the rooftop. I think of the window of sky and my mind goes blue.

He came to the dormitory for the first time a few days after I had arrived. He said that he was lonely, that his wife was cold and ruined by too many children. 'I have been watching you,' he said. 'Is there any shame in feeling desire for a woman?' He sat on the bed and splayed the fingers of his hands against each other. He rested his elbows on his thighs and his pushed-together forefingers pulled at his lip, in the manner of a man trying to solve a difficult problem. 'Let us think of it as a business arrangement,' he said. 'Mutually beneficial. I will help you in exchange for the only thing you have to sell.' The following day I moved my few things from the dormitory into a small room at the back of the hotel.

The other hotel guests treat me with contempt. They pretend to resent me for having a room to myself, for preferential treatment by the hotel owner. But I believe they are humiliated by their powerlessness to intervene. They would rather think me a whore than admit to their own cowardice.

'I saw the Barracuda again today,' says Hamilton. We are sitting on the roof in the evening, after the worst of the dust and the heat have passed. Hamilton turns the pages of a magazine as he speaks. The guests sit facing in the direction of the border. They may or may not be listening.

'He crossed twice. Once in the morning and once in the afternoon.'

Every day Hamilton walks across town to the checkpoint to watch the people coming and going. Sometimes I go with him. He is very quiet at the border. Quiet and intense. He stands in the shade of a billboard, his eyes darting from person to person. The wispy moustache that he has grown makes him look younger, not older as he intends. He lights cigarettes, dropping them to the ground when they are half smoked, grinding them into the dust with his foot and then lighting another. He pretends not to know me.

Eventually he will spot the Barracuda, christened by Hamilton for his sharp face, the long fins of his car. He wears a cream Stetson and suits too heavy for the heat. Hamilton does not know his name or what business brings him to the town so often, but imagines him to be a man of some importance. The border officials greet him with smiles, shake his hand, and then wave him through without looking at his documents. Once Hamilton has spotted him coming across the border, or leaving, he relaxes. His mood improves and he will talk to me about this or that, his latest scheme to get across the border perhaps. He keeps a tally of how many times the Barracuda crosses each week.

Hamilton has tried many times to get across the border. 'From now on my bed will be free,' he announces before leaving the hotel in the middle of the night. A few hours later, or maybe at noon, he returns, limping from some injury, or with cuts to his face or legs. Unchastened, he relates the story, citing some detail or piece of poor luck but for which he would have succeeded. The hotel owner listens in. 'You will never succeed,' he tells Hamilton, 'your methods are too primitive.' Hamilton has tried many different methods. He has tunnelled under the border fence. He has climbed over it and cut through it. He has stolen a uniform and disguised himself as a border guard. Once, he dressed all in green and hid for a night among a truckload of bananas. Overnight the fruit ripened and the border guards picked him from the yellow cargo like a grub.

He has been caught so many times that he is known to all the officials at the checkpoint. That is why often, when he stands under the billboard looking out for the Barracuda, they will grin at him and tip their hats. They do not take him seriously.

'Soon,' says Hamilton to no one in particular, 'I will cross the border as easily as the Barracuda does. I will cross backwards and forwards many times a day.' He takes out the tiny pair of scissors that he keeps in his pocket and carefully begins to cut around a picture in the magazine. Another guest, a big man named Kelman with a scar running down his cheek, gets to his feet. 'And you will wash with champagne,' he says, 'and eat caviar and wipe your arse with silk handkerchiefs.' A couple of the other guests laugh, dry, hard laughs, like stones. Most of us do not. We do not have the heart to mock Hamilton as the border officials do.

'His methods are primitive,' the hotel owner says to me. 'There are better ways,' he says, 'easier ways.' Sometimes, when he is finished with me, he stands at the small window of my room and talks about the town. 'There are opportunities in a town like this, opportunities for a businessman.' He puts his hands together. 'People are like dogs,' he says. 'When a dog is hungry enough it will fight over anything, a crust of bread, a pool of water. And when they fight, they fight each other. They are too stupid to fight the thing that feeds them.' He is right. This is a town of desperate people. People of different skin colour or religion, people who speak different languages, people who are cousins, brothers even, they will argue and fight over small things, a pair of shoes, cigarettes. Sometimes people are killed. The hotel owner turns away from the window. 'This town is full of dogs,' he says.

He has excited himself with this talk and comes back towards the bed. 'But this is different,' he says. 'We have an arrangement, an arrangement that suits us both.' I shiver as his hands trace along my spine. He laughs. 'And I will miss you when you are gone.'

'Please,' said Hamilton, 'please help yourselves to my bed. Soon I will be sleeping on a mattress as soft as water, on pillows stuffed with goose down.' He has been gone for three days. On the evening he left, he boasted of his plan to hide in the trunk of the Barracuda's car. He would follow the Barracuda when he came into town. When he parked and went to do his business Hamilton would pick the lock, he said, no problem, and shut himself in. 'There will be a carpet in there,' he said, 'and I will lie with my hands behind my head. I will hear the greetings of the officials as they wave us through the border. The Barracuda is lucky for me,' he said.

We believe that Hamilton is dead. One man talks hopefully of him having made it to the other side, but the fact of his saying it means he believes it even less than the rest of us. He has finally been killed crossing the border, as we all expected he would be, as perhaps he also expected. Up on the roof there is little talk of it and what there is is casual, unconcerned, callous even. 'Thank God,' says Kelman, 'that

I no longer have to listen to his wretched voice.' But the atmosphere is subdued, the silences long and thick. The heat and the dust of the middle of the day seem less tolerable.

The visits of the hotel owner to my room have become more frequent, his caresses bolder. He is uninhibited now in his demands. It is both less and more terrible because he expects it, I expect it, it is usual. His talk about how and when he will honour his part of our arrangement has become vague, cryptic. 'You will do well across the border,' he repeats instead, and now when he says it, it is not desire in his voice, I think, but mockery. He takes satisfaction, also, in Hamilton's death. 'His methods were too primitive,' he says, and reaches for me with his appalling hands.

On the fourth day Hamilton returns. He sits silently on the roof. He will not say where he has been or explain the burn-like wounds on his hands and arms.

The hotel owner does not linger on the roof to make comments as has been his habit. Perhaps he does not want to acknowledge Hamilton's return. After all, he does not like to be contradicted. 'You,' is all he says, speaking to me, 'I would like to see you downstairs.'

He does not wait to trace his finger along the line of my spine, but pulls me from the bed and turns me against the wall. The wall is cool. Paint has flaked off at the level of my eyes, revealing a piece of plaster the shape of an unknown country or continent. Above is the sound of footsteps and chairs being dragged across the roof garden. The hotel owner's breaths, warm and meaty, come quickly. He is sour today and eager, too eager, to degrade me.

'I am unhappy with our arrangement.' I have twisted

round to face him. His face is close to mine, his mouth open a little, strands of spittle hanging between his lips. 'I am unhappy with our arrangement and I would like to re-negotiate.' Circumstances have made me reckless. But he does not speak and I go on. I tell him that he must provide me with the documents necessary to get across the border, that his visits will be fruitless until he makes the arrangements. I am uncertain if he is listening, if he is able to listen. Still he does not speak. Not of dogs, or business, or how well I will do across the border. He cannot think past the satisfaction that is being denied to him. His need is pitiable, his homeless erection absurd.

Hamilton has not been himself since he returned to the hotel. He makes no boasts. He no longer smokes. He is up on the roof at all times. He is there when I go up in the morning and there still when I return to my room in the evenings. Those who share the dormitory say that he does not sleep in his bed. He does not walk to the checkpoint to watch the people crossing back and forth.

Hamilton's silence is oppressive. We all feel it. The guests face north, towards the border, but Hamilton's presence presses in on us. His silence is corrosive to our fantasies and our hopes. You can sometimes read it in the faces of the other guests, you can tell that they would have preferred him dead.

It is one week since the hotel owner last summoned me down from the roof of the hotel. Now, instead, he visits me at night with the pretext of discussing the progress of my documentation. He has something else in mind too. He is lustful, frustrated, his delicate hands twitchy and covetous. But I am inflexible. I tell him we must stick to our arrangement. I see him contemplating coercion more direct than before, violent scenarios, but he has lost the initiative and anyway does not have the character for it. He leaves, resentful, with nowhere to put his anger.

It is morning and the heat and the dust are rising. For days now no one has left the hotel to try and get across the border. 'You are vandalising hotel property,' the hotel owner tells Hamilton. A magazine is balanced on Hamilton's knees. Its colours are grainy, aged prematurely by the sun. Hamilton is cutting carefully through one of the pages. He does not respond to the hotel owner. 'They are provided for the enjoyment of all my guests. I can no longer tolerate it.'

Someone pushes back a chair and there is the unsympathetic sound of plastic on concrete. 'It is true,' says the big man, Kelman, who stands behind Hamilton. He points at the magazine. 'What if I want a car like this? A house like this? A woman like this?' He leans over and takes the magazine from Hamilton's knees. He holds it by its spine and waves it in the air, as if trying to shake loose something caught between the pages.

'Where are your expensive suits? Your Cuban cigars? Your crushed ice?' Kelman continues to shake the magazine, the dismembered pages hanging in tails and crescents. There is a long time when nothing happens and there is no sound but for the flapping of the pages of the magazine. Then Hamilton bites Kelman's bare leg, just above the knee, and Kelman goes down heavily making a strange noise, something like a sigh. Hamilton picks up the dropped magazine and sits back down in the plastic chair.

Kelman stabs him first in the back of his neck. Then, as Hamilton falls to the floor, again in the back. Kelman rolls him over and I can see each time as he withdraws the tiny shafts of the scissor blades and then drives them back into Hamilton's chest, stomach and face. There is no struggle and it is surprisingly quiet, just Kelman's concentrated grunts, like that of a man chopping wood, and the muted, banal sound of steel pushing into flesh.

There is a thin layer of dust covering Hamilton by the time his body is moved. The hotel owner says something about the heat and the smell and tells two of the guests to carry it down to the street. Someone is flicking vaguely through Hamilton's magazine. The man next to him is wearing Hamilton's shoes. Soon it will be time to go back downstairs. For now I adjust my chair and look across the street in front of the hotel. I look through the gap between the government buildings, and on, towards the blue sky across the border.

The Starving Millions

'NICE CAR,' SAID NICK'S BROTHER ED, AS THEY PUT THE BAGS in the boot at the airport. Nick looked up at him, wondering if Ed meant anything more than this and then deciding that he did not. He would have to try not to be so touchy. They had not seen each other for nearly two years and his brother was simply making an effort. After all, it was a nice car, a black four-wheel-drive Toyota, but hardly ostentatious. It was the first substantial thing Nick had bought when he and Beth had moved to the US eighteen months before and he could not pretend he did not enjoy sitting up high behind the wheel, driving the wide sunny streets on the way to work every day.

'Big,' said his brother.

'Well,' said Nick, starting the engine, 'we have the baby now. And anyway, everything's big out here, you'll see.' He pinched his belly and grinned at Rosie, Ed's wife, sitting in the back. 'Even me.'

'You look well,' she said.

'I'm a fat American, you mean.'

They had never been close but Nick was grateful that Ed and Rosie had made the effort to come to his wedding, especially as it had not been an easy journey. For the last year they had been working on some kind of hospital ship run by a Christian organisation that they were involved with. The ship went up and down the coast of Africa, giving out

treatment and supplies in war-torn or impoverished countries. Nick was vague about the details. He knew that his
brother and Rosie had been given some basic medical
training before they left England but privately he wondered
what on earth use Ed – who had a degree in history – might
be in this situation. Once every few months Nick would
receive a card postmarked from Liberia, the Congo or Angola
with a brief message saying 'both well', 'Africa extraordinary' or mentioning a particular country's 'terrible problems'.
It was always the same card, a picture of *The Angel of Hope*,
a decrepit-looking ship that Nick was certain he would not
be tempted to put to sea in. Ed and Rosie had only finished
on the boat the previous week and to get to the wedding in
time they had flown from Ivory Coast to Paris and then to
London, before catching the plane to Denver.

It was a source of wonder to Nick that he and Ed shared
the same parents and had grown up in the same household
with only three years between them. Although their parents
had been regular churchgoers they had never tried to force
their faith on their sons. With Nick it hadn't stuck and by
his teens he retained only the woolliest notion of a divine
order. But while he experimented with drugs and girls and
politics, his brother spent his university years attending the
chaplaincy and organising events for the Christian Union.
Nick had assumed this was just a phase, a hangover of
adolescent self-consciousness or eccentricity that Ed would
grow out of the same way he had grown out of sucking his
thumb. It didn't happen, and as time went on Nick began
to regard his brother as something of an embarrassment,
the sort of person that at university he would have ridiculed
as painfully earnest and repressed. He told stories of his
brother's piety – never swearing, giving away his Christmas

presents to a charity shop, spending his summer holidays building an orphanage in Bangladesh – and as they lay on a beach in Thailand or thought about buying cocaine, it became customary among Nick's friends to ask, 'But what would St Edward say?'

As soon as they had finished university Ed and Rosie got married and began living and working in a homeless shelter in east London. This led, in time, to the boat. When Nick thought of Ed these days, he often had a vision of him as a dour Victorian missionary, buttoned up in a stiff jacket and collar, striding through slums in searing African heat, clutching his Bible. But Nick also knew that the mockery of his brother hid some other feeling, an unease he had felt in his company for as long as he could remember, the sense that despite everything – his professional success, his new baby, his upcoming wedding – he was fickle, trivial, somehow fundamentally lacking in seriousness. When he had told Ed over the phone that he and Beth had both been offered jobs in Denver, Beth's home town, adding that the money was too good to refuse, he had been almost annoyed when his brother said that it sounded like a good opportunity and wished him luck.

When they got back from the airport Nick showed Ed and Rosie down into the basement of the house where there was a large bedroom, bathroom and second living room. The rooms had never been used by visitors before and as he opened doors and walked them through Nick wondered for a second why they had bought such a large place. They had been able to afford it and at the time that had seemed like reason enough. But his brother and Rosie seemed happy with the arrangement. No doubt they were simply grateful for somewhere comfortable after all their flights and, prior to that, Africa. Thinking of this, Nick reminded himself to ask his brother more about their work and what conditions had been like on the boat. After dumping the bags they went upstairs to talk to Beth, who Ed and Rosie had only met twice before, and be introduced to Katie, Nick's daughter, who had been born since he had last seen his brother.

Ed and Rosie had brought Katie a present, an ugly little doll made out of two sticks bound together and covered in rough material. 'A girl in Sierra Leone gave it to Ed,' said Rosie. 'He helped treat her for an eye infection. It's not very exciting but we thought it was a nice thing to pass on.'

'It's very thoughtful,' said Beth. 'She has so much of this plastic rubbish already.'

Later, Nick drove them all over to Beth's parents for dinner. In the car Ed said, 'Nick, before we forget, what do we owe you for the flights?'

'Nothing at all.'

'Really,' said Ed, 'we'd rather pay for them.'

'Well, unlucky, because they're a present from me.'

'Nick,' said Ed.

'Don't make a big deal out of it, Ed. I already sold my soul so allow me to feel good about myself now and again.' Ed did not reply and so, after a few moments, Nick said quickly, 'Really, I wanted you guys here, don't worry about it.'

Beth's family had flown in from around the country and her mother had cooked an enormous joint of beef. Nick sat talking to Beth's father, Bill, a retired lawyer who he got on with so well that Beth sometimes joked about which member of her family he was really interested in. Nick was at the other end of the table from his brother, but about half an hour into the meal he heard Ed say, apparently in response to something he had been asked, '. . . the real problem is the lack of basic medicines. Most of these things are completely treatable. But as it is you see small children with tumours like this.' Nick looked over at him. Ed had put down his knife and fork and was holding up his hand, making a ring with his thumb and forefinger, almost as if he had the bloodied and malignant lump there in front of him. 'They try and cut them out but they don't have the equipment. The hygiene is so poor that more often than not they die anyway. And that's only the beginning – glaucoma, dysentery, Aids of course . . .'

Ed had been engaged in conversation from across the table by Beth's brother-in-law, Karl, a surveyor from Phoenix who bred bulldogs and who had taken Nick to his first baseball game. Nick looked around the table. Other conversation had died away and everyone was listening to Ed. Nick leaned forward, intrigued to see that his brother had become such an expert. He was about to ask a question when Beth's mother cut in, smiling. 'Perhaps this is a discussion we could save for after dinner.'

'Anyway, I admire you,' said Karl, 'people like you. We don't all get our hands dirty.'

'We don't really see it that way,' said Ed.

'No, of course not. Just a turn of phrase. Are you going back?'

'No,' said Ed, 'not for now.'

'Job done?' Nick said, and then wished he had not. His brother gave no sign of having heard him.

'The project's in some financial difficulty,' Ed said. Karl nodded and, after a pause, changed the subject.

'So, what do you think about your kid brother getting married?'

'Oh no,' said Ed, 'I'm younger.'

'But you beat him to it?'

'Yes, one of the many things I've done to annoy him.'

Karl laughed and Beth's mother offered everyone more food. Talk turned to a ski condo in Vail that Nick, Karl and Bill were planning to go in on three ways. The idea was that it would be a place the whole family could use at the weekends and for holidays. Karl said that apart from anything else, property up there was a gold mine and it would be a guaranteed investment for everyone.

Neither his brother nor Rosie had really touched their food and it occurred to Nick how much weight they had lost since he had last seen them. Rosie had been almost plump at their wedding. Ed, especially, looked gaunt, his eyes large and dark in his face and Nick thought he could be taken for someone ten years older. It all added to his natural air of severity and perhaps this is what it was, a gradual perfecting of an ascetic look he had been working on for years. Perhaps food and good health had become the latest form of self-denial. Or was it, Nick wondered, all out of some bizarre solidarity with the starving millions? Despite their deeply browned skin, he decided, they both looked faintly sick.

As he and Beth were getting ready for bed, Nick complained about his brother. 'He can't ever let it go. I sometimes think he just wants people to feel bad about themselves. It's a kind of meanness. Maybe he'd be happier if we all had tumours.'

'That's a little unfair,' said Beth. 'They've just arrived here from God knows what. It can't be easy to adapt. You should go easy on him.' This was what Nick had expected her to say and he liked it about her, her generosity, part of what he thought of as her Americanness, and it made him glad again that he was marrying her. It struck him particularly because Beth was not in any way like his brother. She was down-to-earth, practical, at home with material and other pleasures, unburdened by things it made no sense to be burdened by. When Ed had written from Africa that he was leading daily prayers on the boat with his guitar they had both nearly wept with laughter at the thought of it. 'Just what they need,' Beth had said, 'the wretched of the earth healed through song.'

'I've been trying to go easy on him for years,' Nick said. 'And I always think it's going to be better when I see him, but it never is.'

Beth got into bed. 'Anyway, he's your brother, you're supposed to be embarrassed by him. If you're worried my family's not going to like him, don't. It doesn't matter.' She laughed. 'Perhaps what you're really worried about is that they'll like him more than they like you.'

Nick grinned. 'As if that were possible.'

'Still, it was sweet of them to get something for Katie.'

'Something is the word for it,' said Nick. 'I can't wait to see what they got us for a wedding present.'

When their parents were killed in a car crash five years before, Nick received a letter from his brother full of religious homilies about death and grief and reassuring him that they had gone to a better place. Ed said that God loved us without reservation and that He had a plan for all of us. At the end he had signed off, 'Yours in Christ, Ed.'

It bothered Nick that Ed thought it necessary to put all this in a letter, rather than saying it over the phone or in person. At the time they were both living in London and seeing each other almost every day to deal with the aftermath of the accident. It struck Nick as fantastically conceited of his brother to believe that what he had to say on the subject was worthy of being written down. Ed, he felt, was trying out a pose, that he had been waiting all along for an event awful enough to match his piety. There seemed to be another implication to the letter too – now that life had revealed itself in all its profundity and suffering, he felt his brother to be saying, shouldn't Nick cast off the pretence of an unbeliever and accept what he in fact knew to be true?

He wanted to tell his brother that he found him ridiculous. For a few minutes after receiving the letter he considered sending Ed a postcard that just said 'Which better place?' or 'Better how?' but in the end he could not bring himself to do it. Instead, it was never mentioned by either of them – conspicuously so, it seemed to Nick – and, looking back, he sometimes felt that this was a victory for his brother.

But following their parents' death it was Ed who held things together. It was Ed who knew what needed doing and, he had to admit, what their parents would have wanted. Ed phoned or wrote to family and friends. He organised the funeral and gave a reading while Nick found he could only nod and mumble at the aged aunts he remembered vaguely from his childhood. Afterwards, Nick made desultory efforts to take charge, feeling that as the eldest these things were somehow his responsibility, but he found much of it intolerable and in the end he consoled himself with the fact that his brother, who was working as a volunteer, had more time. In the following six months Ed arranged the clear-out and sale of their parents' house, and dealt with the execution of the will.

In the period that followed Nick felt as if a weight had been lifted from him, some kind of burden of expectation or judgement that he had not known had existed and which he did not think had much to do with the sort of people they had been. He felt an odd sense of freedom. About a year later he met Beth, an American working in his company, and soon afterwards they had begun to talk about leaving London.

Nick had hoped that his brother would not wish to come on the bachelor night two days before the wedding but when Ed made no sign of opting out Nick took him aside. 'This might not be your thing,' he said. 'I won't be offended if you want to pass on it.'

'Nice try,' said Ed. 'But I think can handle it.'

'Well, you have been warned.'

Karl had organised for a stretch limo to pick them all up from Nick's house, drive them around town long enough to drink a couple of bottles of champagne and then drop them at a bar. Nick felt sorry for his brother. Ed was sitting at the far end of the car, squashed between Ray and Mike, two of Nick's workmates who had been invited along to make up the numbers. The rest of the party were in jeans and shirts, but Ed had worn a suit. It looked old and was rather too large for him and Nick wondered if it had belonged to their father. Nick heard Ray offer to take his brother out duck hunting before the end of his trip.

When the limousine pulled up outside the bar Karl asked for quiet. 'Men,' he said, adopting a sombre tone and looking from face to face, 'listen up. This is serious stuff. Two days from now one more of us gives up his freedom and is lost to the enemy. It is our duty – our privilege! – to make sure that he has one last bite of the apple. So that when he stands up there by the altar he's not thinking about that one last piece of pussy he should have had, that one lovely bit of quim he can't get out of his mind.'

'Like you, you mean,' said Ray.

'No comment,' said Karl, and then bared his teeth.

Nick grinned and rolled his eyes at his brother but Ed was staring up at the roof of the car, one hand tugging gently at the sleeve of his suit. His face was set with a serene expression – irritatingly serene, thought Nick.

In the bar they did shots of tequila. Karl bought round after round and after each slug everyone was encouraged to slam a fist on the bar and exclaim, 'I said goddamn!' After an hour or so they climbed back into the limousine and drove a hundred yards down the street to another bar where they did the same. Nick hardly spoke to his brother. Ed was standing on the edge of the group, sometimes talking to Ray, declining his shots but not, Nick thought, looking like he was having an altogether terrible time.

After one more bar Karl announced that it was time to commence the real business of the evening and the limousine dropped them in the parking lot of a strip club. Above the entrance a huge neon sign showed a cartoonishly shaped woman astride a cannon and below it the words 'Shotgun Willies'. Karl paid for them all to get in, bought two bottles of champagne and a round of sambucas at the bar and then produced several small rolls of five-dollar bills fixed in rubber bands that he handed to each of them. Nick watched his brother raise his hands in refusal but Karl tucked the money into the pocket of Ed's suit, as if he were a mafioso dispensing bribes. 'My gift to you all,' he said. 'Please, it makes me happy.'

Girls in G-strings were dancing on small stages set around the club and Nick went and sat down at one of them. Ray sat down a couple of seats away from him, lit a cigar and laid one of the five-dollar bills that Karl had given them on the stage. The girl came over, put her hands on Ray's shoulders, and began to grind over him in time to the thumping music, letting her hair fall in his face. When she had finished Ray took a long pull on the cigar and tucked the note into the band of her underwear.

Nick wasn't thinking about the girls. For some reason he had been reminded of something his brother had said to him several years ago, at the time of Ed's own wedding, about how he and Rosie planned to raise their children in the Third World. Nick had laughed and said 'Good luck to you', but occasionally since then, and more often since they had had Katie, the idiocy and self-righteousness of this remark would come into his head and fill him with a kind of fury. If he found the right moment and the right mood he would ask if this was still on the agenda.

Nick looked around. Karl was wandering from stage to stage. He would stop and stare for a minute at a girl and then walk on unsatisfied, the roll of notes gripped in his fist and held out slightly in front of him. Nick spotted Ed standing on his own at the bar, holding a drink. He looked so out of place, with his fixed expression and baggy suit, that Nick wouldn't have been entirely surprised if one of the bouncers had asked him to leave. He wondered why Ed had insisted on coming. As it was his presence threw the whole place into a seedy, pitiful light, the girls squirming joylessly in the overheated room, their plastered-on smiles and make-up. This was the effect his brother had on everything, Nick thought.

Ed came over to the stage where Nick was sitting.

'I'm sorry –' said Ed.

'Sorry?' Nick cut in. 'Don't be sorry. What's to be sorry for?' He grabbed his brother's arm and pulled him down into the chair next to him, more roughly than he had intended.

'You know this is all bullshit.' Nick gestured at the stage and the club beyond. 'It's just playing. I don't even like champagne. All bullshit.' He was still holding his brother's arm. 'While I've got you –'

'I'm going,' said Ed. He was holding out the roll of notes that Karl had given him. 'Can you give this back?' Nick took the roll from his brother and laid it on the stage in front of Ed. The girl spotted the money and began to walk over. Ed reached for the notes but Nick gripped his wrist. Now Nick was holding his brother by both arms.

'Don't,' Nick said. 'It's not polite.'

The girl leaned forward and placed her hands on Ed's shoulders. Nick let go of his brother, stood up and walked to the toilets. On the way back he went to the bar and by the time he returned Ed had gone.

A few minutes later Karl herded them back into the limousine and they drove to another club. It was late. The place was smaller and more brightly lit. There were no stages and the girls, who struck Nick as older and less attractive than before, walked around among the few customers who were still there. Nick was tired and starting to feel hung-over. When Karl eventually reappeared from a side room, grinning and holding up his hands to show that he had been relieved of his cash, they left and drove home.

The wedding went off well. It was a beautiful day and everyone, it seemed to Nick, was in an excellent mood.

A vintage Rolls-Royce drove them from the house to the church where they were married and a small choir sang songs that Nick and Beth had chosen. In the previous couple of days Katie had taken to Ed and he was given the job of looking after her during the ceremony. The reception was held in a marquee on the lawns at Beth's parents' house. There was a jazz band, and it was so warm that some of the guests swam in the pool before the meal.

For the first time since Ed had arrived, Nick did not feel anxious about his brother. Occasionally he glanced around and saw him, often in the thick of a group of people, Beth's elderly relatives or friends of her parents, people Nick himself barely knew or recognised. Ed played easily with the younger children too and it occurred to Nick that, against the odds, his brother was proving a credit to him. Several times Nick spotted him in earnest conversation with Karl.

After the meal, Bill got up and spoke. He welcomed Nick into the family and said he couldn't be happier in Beth's choice of husband. Then he introduced Ed, saying that although he was not a scheduled speaker, he had asked to say a few words. For a moment, as his brother stood up, Nick's heart sank.

'Since we arrived here,' said Ed, 'my brother and I haven't had much time to talk. And it's a long time since we've seen each other. So I wanted to take this opportunity to say how glad Rosie and I are to be here and that this is happening. We don't know Beth well but if she is prepared to put up with my brother then she must be something special. I am certain our parents would have approved.'

He paused and took a sip of water. 'Anyway, I know the real point of these speeches is to assassinate the character of the groom and as the person who has known him the longest I take that responsibility seriously.' Ed went on to tell a story Nick had all but forgotten of how, when they were children, Nick offered his brother ten pence if he would stand naked in a window at the top of their house for twenty seconds, while the other children in the neighbourhood played in the street below. Ed hammed the story up, making everyone laugh. Nick felt he had underestimated his brother – perhaps he had always been guilty of underestimating him. Ed explained how, as he stood in the window, Nick had adjusted his seven-year-old brother's arms and legs so that he was fully spreadeagled, and then counted to twenty so slowly that Ed had begun to cry.

It was odd to hear his brother tell this story so vividly. Nick had not been in the habit of thinking of his past and there now seemed so little to connect himself with the person Ed was describing. Beth loved to talk about her childhood, growing up in Colorado in the seventies, her large family and the summer holidays spent with her grandparents on the West Coast. Nick knew her stories back to front. Now that they were living in Denver it was as if her past had come to stand for them both and he sometimes felt a nostalgia for her memories that was entirely absent from his own.

'So two things,' said Ed as he came to the end of the story. 'Firstly, I want to say to Beth that this was all a long time ago and I'm sure that she has nothing to worry about, and secondly to ask' – here he turned to Nick – 'can I have my money now?'

In the days after the wedding, Nick left Ed and Rosie to their own devices. He lent them his car and they drove over to Boulder and then down to Colorado Springs to visit someone they had worked with on *The Angel of Hope*. The day before their flight back to London Karl took them up into the Rockies. They wanted to see the mountains and Karl needed to take a final look at the condo he was buying with Nick and Bill in Vail and run over a few details with the real estate agent. They left early in the morning and Nick was in bed by the time they came in.

The following day Nick loaded Ed and Rosie's bags into the car and they set off for the airport. Ed was in the passenger seat and Rosie sat in the back. Nick switched on the radio, flicked between stations and then turned it off. He could not think what to say to his brother. There seemed something final about the moment, as if an obligation had been fulfilled and now neither of them needed to have anything to do with the other. With their parents dead, they no longer even had family in common. They drove in silence until they reached the freeway.

'So you haven't said much about the mountains,' said Nick. 'How was it up there yesterday?'

'It was beautiful,' said Rosie. 'So peaceful.'

'Great time of year to be up there,' said Nick. 'Any time is a good time, in fact.'

They were silent again for several minutes.

'Did you see the place?' said Nick.

Ed made a sound, either a sigh or a drawing in of breath. Nick looked over at him. Ed put his finger on the button to open the window.

'Yes, we saw it.'

'And what did you think?'

'I should tell you that Karl is making a donation to our appeal for the boat,' said Ed.

Nick looked at the road ahead and then began to nod slowly.

'I see.' He drummed his fingers on the steering wheel. 'I see, I see. And I'm guessing that after this donation there isn't enough left over for the condo.'

'I believe so,' said Ed. 'Karl feels bad about it.'

'Does he? Shouldn't he feel good about it? Wouldn't that be the point?'

Ed didn't reply.

'Do you feel good about it?' Nick said.

Ed turned to look at his brother.

'God loves you, you know. You don't think so, but He does. He loves all of us, regardless.'

'Regardless of what?'

'Regardless of anything.'

'Well, thanks, I'll bear that in mind,' said Nick. 'But what I'm really interested in is what kind of money are we talking here?'

'It's not for me to say. Enough to help us carry on with our work.'

'Spreading His word?'

'Yes, that's part of it.

'I'm a bit confused,' said Nick. 'So which is the most important part? Helping the needy or bringing them to God?'

'It's part of the same thing. Many do convert, if that's what you want to know. I'm sorry you resent me, Nick.'

'Oh Christ, don't be a jerk.' Nick slammed the palm of his hand on the top of the steering wheel and the car veered to the left. His mind was racing. He wasn't sure what was the most important thing to say. 'You're cynical, Ed. You think you're not but you are. You're really cynical. You don't know these people. They're nothing to do with you. You've no right.'

'I'm sorry you can't have your condominium.'

'It's not about the fucking condo.'

'Can you slow down please?' said Rosie. Nick looked at the dial and then braked. They were nearly at the airport.

'Sorry,' Nick said.

No one spoke. Then Ed said, 'Can I ask you something, Nick?'

'Sure, anything you like. Be my guest.'

'Do you miss our parents?'

Nick hesitated. If he was honest, he thought of them less and less, but he did not know how else you were supposed to be. 'Look, Ed. I'm healthy and my family are healthy. I live in a nice house. I just got married and I sleep well at night. Which part of it do you want me to feel guilty about?'

They were at the airport. Nick parked the car and they unloaded the bags.

'Well,' said Ed, 'come and visit.'

'Where?' said Nick.

Ed shrugged. 'We'll see.'

'Thanks, Nick,' said Rosie. 'It was a lovely wedding.'

When they had gone Nick drove the car round to where he could watch the planes taking off. As his brother had been speaking at the wedding, Nick had remembered a game they had invented together as children. They called it 'Having Trouble Breathing'. One of them would lie on a bed with a pillow on his face while the other sat on top of it. The challenge was to lie there as long as possible before crying out, 'Having Trouble Breathing.' Nick remembered the woozy feeling that would come over him and the thrill of not giving in too soon. On one occasion Nick had lain there not moving after Ed had got off, staying dead still while his brother began to scream and shake him.

Nick sat and watched the planes until he decided on one that might have been his brother's. He watched it climb into the sky and disappear. Then he started the car and drove home.

I HAD TWO PATIENTS BOOKED IN FOR THE AFTERNOON. THE first, Mary, I had been seeing once a fortnight for several months. She had made good progress and our sessions were relaxed and informal. A schizophrenic with a history of self-harm and suicide attempts, she had gradually reduced her medication and was now planning to move out of a hostel and into her own flat. We discussed the issues that were worrying her about living independently but overall she said she was feeling optimistic about the future. At the end of the session she asked me if I had a family. Because it seemed cruel to suddenly insist on the boundaries of our relationship – and because my happiness did not seem anything to be coy about – I told her that I was married and that my wife, June, was three months pregnant. I said that we were going for the first antenatal scan later that day. Mary told me that she hoped to have a family one day and I said there was no reason why it shouldn't happen. After she had gone I left the office and went outside for a cigarette. It was a bright, gusty spring afternoon and I watched the clouds colliding and morphing into new shapes. Back in the building I made coffee and sat down with the file of my second appointment of the day, a new patient.

I had just begun to read when there was a soft knock at the door. I looked up at the clock. It was five to the hour.

'Come in,' I called, a little flustered that I had not had time to go through the notes.

He was short, perhaps five foot six, and probably weighed not more than eight or nine stone. His small frame was swamped by an enormous tracksuit and brand-new, bright red trainers. He wore a baseball cap bearing the words 'Harvard University', which he took off to reveal a closely shaved head. I saw immediately that he was a wreck. His body was hunched over itself and visibly tense. His dark eyes were sunk deep in their sockets and his gaze was both anxious and strangely hypnotised, as if he were only dimly aware of what was going on around him.

I turned to the file. His name was Jetmir Jelenik – or JJ – a Kosovan refugee, and he had been in the UK for eighteen months. He had left Kosovo when his village was attacked by Serbian police. They had taken his mother, father and two brothers away. JJ was badly beaten but left behind. He had been unable to contact his family and now believed they were dead.

Since he had arrived in the country, JJ had complained of pains throughout his body. Scars from the beating were present on his arms, legs and back, but hospital tests had discovered no physiological problem. He had been prescribed painkillers, then a range of antidepressants, but none of these had afforded him much relief. A brain scan offered no neurological explanation and his GP had referred him to me, a clinical psychologist, for treatment.

I looked up at him. 'Well, JJ. I understand you've not been feeling well.'

He nodded.

'You have pains . . .'

'Yes,' he said, quickly, 'terrible pains. Please help me, doctor.'

'I'm not a doctor,' I said, 'not exactly, but of course I will try to help you. Tell me about the pains.'

'They come and go. One day I am OK and the next day my back hurts and I cannot get out of bed. Or I have a headache so bad it makes me sick.'

'Are they just in these places – in your back and your head?'

'No. They can be anywhere. In my hands or in my teeth. In my legs or my feet. Everywhere. What is wrong with me?'

'I hope we can find out.' I tried to smile reassuringly. 'Can you tell me about what happened before you came to this country?'

He nodded vaguely, as if this was a disappointment, and began to repeat what I already knew. His English was excellent but I had the sense of a switch being flicked on. The fluid recall of details and flatness of his voice suggested a story told many times before and the effect was to render the terrible events prosaic. His use of banal emotional qualifiers – 'I was scared', 'I was upset' – only heightened this impression. It was unsurprising. He had no doubt spent much of the last eighteen months repeating his story to immigration officials, benefits agencies, doctors and social workers, many of whom were simply eager to pass him on to a bureaucracy other than their own. It had become a uniform he had to wear to identify himself and I suspected that the automatic litany he repeated – his mother's pleading with soldiers, his father's weeping, his own savage beating with rifle butts – had entirely detached itself from the memory of the events themselves. As he spoke his hands pulled and twisted at his cap.

Then, abruptly, he changed the subject. 'People do not believe me about the pains. They ask me questions because they think I am lying. They want to send me back to Kosovo.'

'You don't want to go back?'

'On no,' he said, alarmed. 'I must not go back.'

'Well, I believe you,' I said. I had an urge to reach out and touch his arm, to comfort him. 'I believe your pains are real.'

In the maternity clinic I held June's hand and we watched the improbable image of our baby twitch and shift on the monitor. The nurse pointed to different parts of the screen and explained that all the internal organs were fully formed and that it was already growing fingernails, eyelashes and hair. She showed us the line of the spine, a hazy density of light that made me think of the Milky Way, and the pulsing blur that was its heartbeat. I watched June watching the screen. She struck me as something extraordinary, and very beautiful. We listened to the nurse and nodded and smiled at this whole new world opening up to us.

It was our first child. We had been trying since our wedding and had begun to worry that it might not happen. Many of our friends said they did not want children. They made what seemed to me trite and self-indulgent remarks about bringing other human beings into 'a world like this', even though they had mostly had comfortable lives. Some changed their minds, of course, but we were never this way. The night we met, and before we had so much as kissed, we spoke of wanting to have a family – I suppose it was part of what attracted us to each other. It is hard to explain the desire for a child. No doubt it has much to do with one's own childhood – wanting to replicate or redeem – but, despite the work I do, it has always seemed too fundamental to make me want to examine it. I knew that since we discovered June was pregnant I had felt, in some indefinable way, that I was more a part of the world, somehow more substantial.

As we drove out of the hospital after the scan I noticed JJ waiting at the bus stop. He was a ridiculous sight in his vast and shiny tracksuit, trainers and baseball cap and I thought of pointing him out to June. Then I imagined him travelling back alone on the bus to a bare, comfortless room. I had treated people from the unit where he lived before and had an image of the shared strip-lit kitchens and vinyl floors, the inoffensive watercolours framed on the walls and the televisions blaring in every room.

I began the next session, a fortnight later, by asking JJ to describe his pains. He seemed not to understand.

'Is it like an ache? Or a sharp pain? A rawness?'

'Yes.'

I looked at him. 'All of those things?'

He shrugged and looked away.

'JJ, what do you think is wrong with you?'

He shrugged again.

'Are you angry?'

'I don't know.'

'You don't know if you're angry?'

'Angry with who?'

'With the people who beat you and took your family? Perhaps you're even angry with them, with your family.'

He looked blankly at me and did not reply.

★   ★   ★

We met every two weeks and each time I tried in different ways to get him to talk. I felt simply that his pains were psychosomatic, a product of the trauma of his beating and separation from his family, that we would be able to unlock them by examining his experiences and his feelings. After two months we were still making no progress. He resisted every tack and it was clear he could not see the point in any of this. I was not a doctor who could carry out measurable tests or give him medicine. All I did was make him talk about things he did not wish to talk about. At times, through his indifference, he seemed to be regarding me with a kind of curiosity, and I saw that with my questions and my meditation tapes I struck him only as obscure, an irrelevance.

'Why do you come to see me?' I asked him in one session when we had come to a halt.

'I don't know,' he said. 'I have to see a lot of people.' Of course he had no choice – it was a condition of his accommodation.

There was no improvement in his physical state. In fact, JJ claimed his pains were getting worse, and more constant. To look at him, this certainly seemed to be the case. His posture had become even more hunched over, his skin sallow and tightly drawn around his face, and throughout our sessions his right foot would keep up a constant anxious jiggling against the floor.

My own feelings had become complicated. It was a mixture of profound pity – he was so young, his circumstances so awful – and growing impatience. I felt at times that he was being stubborn, pointlessly obstructive, or even, in his passivity, mocking my efforts to help him. I brooded on him outside work. I imagined him lying on his bed, staring at the wall or at the ceiling, counting the hours until it was time to eat again. Or aimlessly walking the run-down streets of the neighbourhood near the unit, his tracksuit hanging in folds around him. I thought of the smell of bleach and air freshener, visits to the residents' office to collect medication or get access to money, the laboured jollity of the staff – the utter strangeness and foreignness of it all.

I saw that I was becoming too close to it. I should have made some excuse and referred him on, but this seemed like a failure – and a betrayal of JJ. Towards the end of our sixth session, during which he had sat almost doubled over in his chair, the banging of his foot against the floor signalling an even greater than usual agitation, he said desperately: 'Please help me. I am suffering. I don't want to be in pain any more.'

I nodded to acknowledge him and asked another question. He did not seem to hear me. The violent movement of his leg rattled the chair against the wall behind.

'Please stop that,' I said and grasped his chair with both hands.

He looked up, not shocked by my outburst, but a little bewildered, and I saw once again, very clearly, that he had no real idea who I was or what I wanted from him.

JJ did not turn up for our next session two weeks later. I sat waiting for half an hour before locking up my office and heading out to the car. The unit where he lived was only fifteen minutes from the hospital. It was a dispiriting part of town. A mix of vacant shopfronts and grubby newsagents lined the road and grim-faced estates stretched away on either side. Further on and set back from the main road, the place itself was sterile and well ordered, an anonymous huddle of buildings painted cream and set around a concrete courtyard.

At the office I explained who I was and asked if JJ was in his room. The woman on duty told me that he had been ill for several days. Someone had been supposed to call the hospital to let me know he would not be able to attend his appointment. I asked if I could see him and although it was perhaps unusual to have someone pursuing a patient to their bedside the woman did not query it. 'Hang on a minute,' she said. 'I'll take you up myself.'

Dangling a large set of keys from her hand, she led me across the courtyard and through a door. Inside the building the walls were painted a pale hospital green and bare except for fire extinguishers, smoke alarms and speakers and handsets for an intercom system. Every so often there was a noticeboard with posters advertising upcoming trips to the cinema, or to go ice skating or bowling. For a second I was struck by a bizarre image of JJ lying sprawled at the centre of an ice rink. We went along a series of corridors, through heavy fire doors and up several flights of stairs. 'It's a bit of a labyrinth, I'm afraid,' she said.

We passed a number of the residents in the corridors and to each of them my guide called out a cheerful hello, asked them how they were or reminded them to come to the office later on for one reason or another. Through one open door I saw a very overweight man in pyjamas standing by a cooker, frying something on the hob. JJ's room was at the far end of a corridor. The woman rapped on the door and called out his name. When there was no response she knocked again and then pushed the door open.

'JJ,' she said, 'visitor for you.' She turned to me and rolled her eyes, a gesture that might have seemed callous but instead relieved some of the tension I was feeling. 'I'll leave you to it, then.'

The room was much as I had pictured it. The curtains were drawn but in the dim light I could still see what was there: a narrow bed along one wall, an empty bookcase and a wardrobe. The room was a good size and the way that the furniture was crowded into one corner gave it an odd, temporary feel. It was modern and seemed clean, but the air was musty, a smell of unwashed bodies or stale water. It was also neat – there was none of the chaos or debris that I associated with a seventeen-year-old. The only sign of who occupied the room, or that it was occupied at all, was a glossy picture of a woman Sellotaped on the wall above the bed, apparently torn out of a magazine.

JJ was lying in bed under a blanket and one tracksuited arm hung limply down towards the floor. His cap was on the bedside table. He made an effort to push himself into a sitting position but quickly gave up and lay back down. He did not look at me.

'They said they would telephone you,' he said.

He thought I had come to reprimand him for missing his appointment.

'It's fine,' I said. 'You haven't done anything wrong. I was just concerned.' There were no chairs so I sat down on the edge of the bed. I looked around the room again. I looked back at JJ. His body was so slight that it barely made any shape under the blanket. I recognised one of the meditation tapes I had given him sitting on the bedside table next to his cap. What was I doing here? Was I here because I was concerned about him? Because I felt guilty about the way I had behaved at our last session and wanted to make amends? Had I intended to conduct the session as planned, with JJ lying in the bed in front of me? I did not know.

'How are you feeling?' I said to fill the silence and cover my confusion.

'How long have you been in bed?'

He did not reply to this either. His eyes were flicking around the room and I could see the blanket trembling with the motion of his leg. The atmosphere in the room seemed thick with despair.

I sat there for what must have been several minutes, then got up and left.

As I walked across to the car, the woman who had shown me to JJ's room came out of the office, putting her coat on. Recognising me, she smiled mock sympathetically.

'Productive?'

I rolled my eyes and she laughed.

'Do you need a lift somewhere?' I said.

I told her where I was going and she said I could drop her on the way. Once we were in the car she held out her hand. 'I'm Karen, by the way.'

We did not speak as I pulled out of the car park and onto the main road but as we waited at the first junction I asked her if she had time for a drink.

She looked at her watch. 'Sure. There's a place on the next corner.'

The pub was a dive, a rough all-day and all-night sort of place. It was only four in the afternoon but it was crammed with drinkers and the harsh lighting gave it a sickly, relentless feel. It was a long time since I had been anywhere like it and I felt self-conscious in my shirt and trousers. I went and sat at the only free table, next to a boarded-up window, while Karen went to the bar. When she came back I lit a cigarette and offered her one but she got out her own.

'So how long have you been working there?' I said.

'Long enough that I can't remember.' She dragged on her cigarette and then blew out the smoke.

'Do you like it?'

'I think I'm good at it. I suppose that sometimes feels like the same thing. It's hardly my dream. I don't plan on being there my whole life.'

'What is your dream?'

She laughed. 'I can hardly tell you that. I don't even know you.' She took another drag on her cigarette and then stubbed it out, half smoked. 'But seriously,' she said, 'it's OK. Pretty basic stuff really. Making sure they look after themselves a bit, that they get all the benefits they're entitled to, that they're going to all their doctors' and social workers' appointments, that the only drugs they're taking are the ones prescribed to them.' She laughed again and lit another cigarette. 'We tend to treat them like children, really. Telling them off if they misbehave, giving them rewards if they don't. They are children in a way. They've been ill for so long, most of them, that they're used to being dependent. You get the odd success story, but mostly they just get passed around the system, getting slightly better, slightly worse, going in and out of hospital. Your man JJ – he's one of the better ones. I imagine he's only there because he's a refugee and someone thought they could use his medical condition to get a roof over his head.'

'He's not at all well,' I said.

'You should see some of the others.'

She smiled and tapped her empty glass.

We had another drink and then I drove Karen back to the

block of flats where she lived. 'Nice to meet you,' she said, as she opened the car door. There was a hesitation between us and she turned slightly back towards me. For a moment it seemed like it would not happen and then she leaned over and kissed me hotly on the mouth.

We saw each other about once a week, usually in the afternoons when Karen wasn't working and I had managed to rearrange my appointments. We would meet at the pub, a friendlier and less intimidating place than it had at first seemed. Then, after a few drinks we drove back to hers. By about five o'clock it was over and I would leave to go home or back to the hospital.

I had the impression that Karen was used to having relationships like this, although this may just have been a fantasy of my own inexperience. She was practical and matter-of-fact about all of it: the arrangements to meet, the sex, the gaps when we did not see each other. I told her about June, although I could not bring myself to say that she was pregnant. She was good and easy company but gave very little away. She did not attribute feelings to it. She would not say 'I like you' or 'I've missed you' or 'I want to see you'. Any of this would have seemed inappropriate in what was going on between us. I did not think it concealed any great build-up of feelings for me, just that she had got into the habit of being guarded about herself. She had a young daughter, whose toys and clothes were strewn about her flat, and with a full-time job had no room in her life for difficult or chaotic emotion. She asked little about my life. This was not, I think, because she thought it was taboo, but because her own was real and absorbing enough.

For me it was all new and unexplored territory. I moved

around in a kind of daze, learning the habits and rituals of a life that was fundamentally altered. Everything was terribly heightened, even the most trivial action or observation – the closing of the car door to go up to Karen's flat, the sight of the clouds moving across her window. And this was not just during the time spent with Karen. As I sat waiting for a patient or smoked a cigarette in front of the building everything I looked at and felt was sharp and vivid; every moment seemed invested with a new weight.

Yet I adapted my life to it with a kind of ruthlessness and efficiency, as if I had all the time being carrying around this capacity inside me. Without a second thought I would rearrange my appointments so that I could make our meetings. At Karen's I showered with my own soap and then checked my clothes and the car for anything that might incriminate me. On one occasion I phoned June from Karen's flat to say that I had a departmental meeting and would be late home. I watched myself doing these things – kissing and talking and lying in bed with another woman – and was astonished at the ease with which they occurred.

It was remarkable how much this life, in all its strangeness and turmoil, resembled the one I had previously been leading. Everything was different and yet, aside from my weekly betrayal, nothing was. June and I saw friends and family and attended hospital appointments and antenatal classes. We made arrangements for the birth and met the midwife. I cleared out the spare room and began to turn it into a nursery. We shopped for things the books told us we would need. June's belly continued to swell.

But I could no longer see June and I clearly. I had lost all sense of the future, the vision which I realised I had been nursing since before we were married: June and I and our child in our house, the baby learning to walk and speak. Now when I tried to look ahead, the future was blurred, indistinct. Only the present was astonishingly vivid. I could no longer imagine what it would feel like to be a parent, the husband to a mother. It sometimes came to me with a sense of dull surprise that I would soon be a father. When we discovered that we were having a boy, I had to fake a reaction.

At the same time, and despite all I did to conceal my affair, I was constantly seized by the urge to confess. As we sat at dinner, or drove, or walked in the park, I would be on the verge of it, picking out the words I would say, arranging and rearranging them. 'June,' it went, 'there's something I need to tell you. June, I don't know how to say this.' It was a heady, compulsive feeling, imagining these words coming out, but the clichés of such a confession made it seem unreal, false, and I could not go through with it.

It began to seem as if the possibility of confession, the exposure and what came after, was at the heart of what I was doing, the concealed motive. It was not lust or discontent that had led me to this – I felt neither of those things. No, it was not that.

I would lie awake in bed at night, my mind racing. One night June woke to find me watching her.

'What's the matter?'

'Nothing,' I said. 'Go back to sleep.'

But the words were so loud it seemed astonishing that she could not hear them. 'June,' it rang in my head, 'there's something . . . June . . .' And the thought of it seemed like the most extraordinarily sweet relief.

* * *

Two weeks after I visited JJ in his room he arrived at my office for his usual appointment. Neither of us mentioned our previous encounter and after that our sessions followed the usual pattern. I asked him how he had been feeling and he described his pains. We discussed his family, their abduction and his own beating. We went over and over the same ground but I no longer had any faith in the idea that he would improve. I could only see him degenerating. I think that I expected him to die. We had been over his past so many times that it had begun to lose its distinctness. When I thought of what had happened to him and where he was from it appeared to me as a dim blur of uniforms, guns and violence, everything wreathed in hopelessness. Perhaps this was why it took me so long to notice that he was, as it turned out, recovering. He had to draw my attention to it himself.

'Next week I start a computer course,' he said at the beginning of one of our sessions, apparently out of the blue. 'Programming. I want to get a job.'

I was taken aback. I had never heard him speak of the future, let alone in a positive way. Then, in a sudden rush, I saw that all the signs had been there, but that I had somehow made myself oblivious to them. Several times over the past few sessions he had mentioned another resident at the unit, someone with whom he seemed to have made friends. They had been going shopping and to the cinema together. I glanced at the file and saw that I had made notes of all this and yet had not registered the significance of it. Now that I observed him more carefully I saw that he looked different too. I had written in the file that he had bought new clothes – jeans and a jacket – but I had not noticed how much of a better fit they were, how much they changed the impression he made. I looked and saw that his foot tapped the floor with only a slow steady pulse.

'Do you have any pains today?' I said.

'Only a little,' he said, 'here in my leg.'

'What about yesterday?'

'The same. A little in my leg. I am trying not to think about them.'

He did not arrive for his next appointment. I thought perhaps he had deteriorated again, that he was too ill to get himself to the hospital. I wondered if I had been mistaken about his improvement or overestimated it in my eagerness to see him better. It seemed very possible that I had gone from one extreme to another, from imagining him dying to being convinced that he was almost recovered. My own judgement seemed fractured, unreliable, and now a whole variety of things flashed through my mind – that he had had some kind of accident, that he had been deported, even that he had killed himself.

This time when I arrived at the unit I did not go to reception. One of the doors off the courtyard stood ajar and I went through it into the building. The layout of the place was as confusing as before and this time I did not have a guide. The same arrangement of rooms and corridors was repeated from block to block and from floor to floor and there was little to distinguish one from another. Eventually I arrived on what I felt to be JJ's corridor. The overweight man in pyjamas that I had seen on my last visit was coming out of the bathroom, trailing a towel behind him.

I walked to the end of the corridor and knocked on the door. There was no reply so I knocked again and then opened it. The room was as I remembered it, the furniture all huddled in one corner, but there was no sign of anyone living there. The picture above the bed was gone. It smelled as if it had been freshly cleaned. The curtains were drawn but the window behind them was open and they flapped gently in the wind.

A feeling of acute desolation came over me and I sat down on the end of the bed, as I had done weeks before when I had first come looking for JJ. Then it occurred to me that I had come to the wrong room, perhaps on the wrong floor, and that it was an exact replica of the one directly above or below it. When I went downstairs and knocked on the door of the equivalent room, the young woman who opened it had no idea who JJ was. I tried to describe him but I could see I was making her nervous. On the top floor I tried again but no one answered.

I began to go from door to door, asking the person who answered if they knew which room JJ was in. A few of them pointed vaguely along a corridor or to another part of the building. Others did not understand what I wanted or simply shut the door. It was Karen who eventually found me, sitting on the floor in one of the kitchens, disorientated and tearful. A few of the residents I had disturbed had gathered in the corridor to watch, and Karen led me quickly from the building. She told me that JJ had moved out two days before, into his own flat. A week earlier he had found out that his asylum application had been successful and that he would not be sent back to Kosovo.

Karen and I only met on two more occasions. We did not make a decision to stop seeing each other but it was clear that a line had been crossed. She had dealt with my visit to the unit discreetly and there had been no fallout for either of us, but we had both had a glimpse of the problems I might have caused. We only referred to it directly at our next meeting when she commented that I had been acting more like one of the residents than one of the professionals employed to help them. On that occasion we went back to her flat but it had an unmistakably valedictory feel and we did not linger in bed as had been our habit. The next time we met, a week later, Karen only stayed for a drink and then said she had things to do. I protested weakly but as soon as she left I realised I was relieved. Perhaps I had come to my senses, and the reflection of myself that I saw in her – of infidelity, and now of professional folly – was not something I could tolerate. To her, I suppose, I had ceased to be the casual affair without consequences. We did not see each other again.

June is due any day now. She is blooming, as they say. Everything is ready – the bag for the hospital is packed and waiting by the door. I have finished decorating the nursery. We have decided on a name. Our lives are lived in the grip of anticipation.

The future seems alive and something to look forward to. What happened with Karen no longer makes any sense in the context of our lives. At times the memory brings a sharp twinge, an almost physical pain, but it quickly passes. Sometimes, when we are out together and the whole city seems full of children and their parents, I like to think that June knows more than she lets on and has forgiven me anyway.

Last week we went to the hospital for a final check-up before the birth. I left June in the waiting room and went outside for a cigarette. It was bright and gusty, a day like the one six months earlier when I had my first session with JJ, although then it was spring and now it is autumn. At that moment I saw him, crossing the square fifty metres away from me. He was leaning into the wind, his cap pulled down over his face, one hand gripping his jacket tightly around him. I had forgotten how slight he was and it seemed that at any time the wind might lift him off his feet and toss him up into the air. He was approaching the main hospital building and I wondered what appointment he could be attending. I called out to him but the sound of my voice was blown back towards me. I started to run but by the time I arrived in the foyer he had disappeared into the streams of people, and was gone.

I.

THE ISLAND IS NOT LARGE, ABOUT A MILE FROM END TO END, the shape of a cashew nut. The shore is rocky except for the small pebbled beach on the inside curve of the nut, where they landed three months ago. The land rises and falls in a way that the conscript, in his letters to his sweetheart, has described as hills, although he knows it to be an exaggeration. The land is not – has never been – cultivated. The soil is dark and hard and for the most part there are only a few shrubs and bushes so nondescript that he would be surprised if they even had names. At one end, however – the southern end? – there is a copse of trees. Here he has dug a toilet. The island is the kind of place, the conscript has often thought, where you might find the fossilised remains of a dinosaur.

The day of the invasion was triumphant. They had argued boisterously about the exact centre of the island and then planted the flag. He still remembers how vivid, how bold, its colours were against the grey sky, the brown earth. That evening they built a fire and roasted a pig that had been brought in anticipation of the mission's success. There was drinking and rowdy singing. The senior officers told stories of other battles, other campaigns, in which they had played roles. In the morning everyone had sore heads and wasted no time in packing up their equipment. He watched them, packed into the flotilla of brightly coloured fishing boats, until they disappeared from the horizon.

2.

The conscript is serious about his duties. He sits now, at dawn, in his camp and takes apart his gun. He lays out the parts, the barrel, the trigger mechanism, the handle, the cartridge compartment and the sight. He pours fluid from a tiny bottle onto a soft cloth and, beginning with the barrel, carefully cleans each component. For the inside of the barrel, and other parts he cannot get to with his fingers and the cloth, he has pipe cleaners. He is thorough and takes his time. He handles it delicately, reverently, as if it were a woman, or a child. Then he reassembles it, oils the trigger mechanism and ensures that the sight is aligned to the barrel. The gun is a new model, imported from overseas. It has only ever been his gun. It smells of its newness, and has never been fired.

In the past month the conscript has learned the value of ritual and routine. Alone on the island, it would be easy to become lazy or careless in his habits, but it is in precisely situations such as this, his training has taught him, that he must remain efficient and alert.

After he has cleaned his gun he runs once around the island. Every hundred yards of the course he has marked a rock with a cross of boot polish. He has a rule that he must touch each of these rocks as he runs, so that he is not tempted to cut corners. It takes him nineteen and a half minutes to run round the island. Or it used to until a week ago when his watch stopped. Now he has a new system. This morning, before he sets off on his run, he builds a fire and puts a pan of water on to boil. When he gets back, breathless, he is pleased to see the water simmering, bubbles rising like drops of mercury from the bottom of the pan to the top. He knows that if he had not maintained a good speed the water would have been boiling by the time he returned. Equally, if there are no bubbles, the water is still calm, then he has run too quickly. It is the consistency which is important to him.

There is something reassuring about his ability to run round the island in this time. He feels that it gives him a certain authority over the territory to which he has been assigned. Now it does not take him nineteen and a half minutes to run round the island. It takes the time it takes to bring the water to a simmer. It is arbitrary, he knows, but it is something.

Once he has caught his breath he walks to the pebbled beach and takes off his uniform. He folds the clothes and puts them in a neat pile beyond the level of the high tide. He places his boots next to his clothes. As he walks down the beach he looks forward to the shock of the freezing water on his skin. He washes carefully. He gets the dirt out from under his finger and toenails. He is as thorough with himself as he is with his gun.

3.

The maps and information he was given prior to the invasion refer to and describe Island 21. There was no information regarding Islands 1 to 20 or 22 and above. He is curious, now, about the existence of these islands, though at the time he had not thought to ask.

The sun is high and hot. The conscript sits in his uniform and scrolls through the dial on his short-wave radio. He would like to hear news about the progress of the military campaign or the election that was imminent when he left the mainland. Occasionally he hears words in the language and accent that is familiar to him. He cranes his head towards the speaker, the muscles of his face tensed, but the voices are quickly blotted out by a rising distortion. He is able, of course, to pick up the incomprehensible voices and music of foreign radio stations. For these the reception is perfect.

He tries to write a letter to his sweetheart. When he first arrived on the island his letters were high-spirited, describing in meticulous and enthusiastic detail the geography of the island and his daily routine. Also, he would write down erotic fantasies that he had dreamed up involving his sweetheart, things that he would never have dared to suggest or describe to her in person. But today, when he tries to write his letter, all he has are questions, banal questions: *How is the weather with you? Is there a new government? Is your mother's health still poor?* And he squirms and gasps out loud when he remembers the appalling scenarios that had titillated him only a few days ago.

He writes *First of all, let me apologise for my long absence.* He pauses. He writes *The sun is high and hot.* Just then the flag flying above the camp catches his eye and he is reminded that it needs patching. After a minute he puts the letter away in a wooden box. He takes out the small bottle of fluid, the soft cloth and the pipe cleaners, and begins to clean his gun.

4.

The conscript is wearing only his starched white regulation underpants and waiting for the water to boil for his morning tea. His uniform is drying on the beach. After his morning run (when he had returned to the camp he had been disconcerted to find the water boiling furiously in the pan) he had bathed in the sea and then decided to wash his uniform. He had used stones to scrub it clean and then laid the pieces out flat on the beach. He had brought his boots to a deep shine and then placed them next to the uniform.

He is not boiling the same water that he heated during his run round the island. He knows that tea should not be made with water that has already been boiled. He cannot remember if he read this somewhere or if someone told him – his mother perhaps, or his sweetheart? – and nor, when he asks himself, does he remember the reason why. Whatever the source, the accuracy, of this piece of information, it has hardened into a truth, an article of faith. He makes his tea with fresh water.

When the water is boiled and he has made the tea, he adds a little sugar. The conscript is very particular about how much sugar he adds. If there is too little he cannot bear the bitterness. If there is a fraction too much it becomes too sickly for him to drink. He begins by adding far less than he knows he needs. Then he sips it and adds a little more. If it becomes too sweet he throws the tea away – the liquid arcs through the air before disappearing into the earth – and makes another cup. Today he only has to make three cups before he has one that he can drink.

His bowels are loosened pleasantly by the tea and instead of going to the beach to put his uniform back on he walks to the copse of trees at one end of the island to relieve himself. He begins to read the thriller that he has already finished many times while sitting here. He enjoys it more each time he reads it. The plot fits together well, like a jigsaw, or a machine, and everything in it that happens, happens for a reason. There is action and intrigue and the characters are full of recognisable virtues. However, each time he has read it he has become more and more frustrated at the book's ending, which he considers a betrayal of the whole story. Last week he wrote a letter to the author expressing this opinion. He has even considered rewriting the final chapter himself. He has a very clear idea of how it should go.

Sometime later he arrives at the pebbled beach and finds that his uniform – his freshly cleaned clothes and shiny boots – are gone. A faint impression shows where the heavy waterlogged material had lain, the shape of a headless man.

5.

It is several days – three? four? – since his uniform disappeared. At the time he had considered, briefly, what might have happened – the wind perhaps, or a freak wave, even a mischievous seabird – but he has refused to let this setback interfere with his duties. Today, as every day since his arrival on the island, he marches up and down in front of his camp. He marches thirty paces and then turns and marches thirty paces in the opposite direction. He marches back and forth twenty times and then comes to a halt facing north, his gun cocked.

Later, the conscript watches curiously as the sun begins to spread along the line of the horizon. At first he cannot explain his interest to himself. Then, just as it disappears into the water, he realises than the sun has set in what he had imagined to be the east. For how many days has he been marching facing the wrong direction? For how long had he been marching up and down behind his camp instead of in front of it? In truth his orders had not stated that the threat would come from a particular direction. He had only assumed.

Now that the sun is gone he feels a little cold, sitting only in his underpants. He wraps himself in the flag that they had planted to mark the invasion of the island. It covers him adequately but the material is thinner and scratchier than he would have expected.

6.

The conscript is composing a letter to his sweetheart. He feels he has something to say but he cannot find the right tone. He cannot even begin. *My darling*, he tries. *Dearest. My love.* Shortly, he folds the unfinished letter and places it in the wooden box with all the other letters he has written to his sweetheart and the letter he has written to the author of the thriller. He picks up his gun and writes in the earth with the barrel. *Sweetheart. Island. Conscript.* He breaks the words down. *Sweet-heart. Is-land. Con-script.* He breaks them down and wonders about secret meanings. He suspects them of conspiracies. He says them aloud, again and again, until they become strange, empty. He stares at them, written in the earth, until they are no more than hieroglyphs.

The conscript sits down and tries to picture his sweet-heart. He has a phrase, *her heart-shaped face*, which he thinks is from a poem or a song. He repeats it to himself but he is no longer sure if it is appropriate and it evokes no image. Nevertheless, he continues. He licks his lips so that they are wet, as if from kissing or being kissed. In his palm the soft cloth that he uses to clean his gun covers the calluses of his hands. He holds himself delicately, awkwardly. The hand explores nervously, unsure of its skill. He does not look at the arm or the hand. He closes his eyes. He imagines it to be the hand of his sweetheart.

7.

The conscript wakes early after a troubled night. He feels that he has dreamed many dreams but he can only recall one – dark liquid arcing through the air and disappearing into the earth, over and over. He is anxious, jumpy, and when the sun comes up he believes he knows the reason why.

On the horizon, coming in and out of view, is another piece of land, another island. He sits and stares as the dawn breaks behind it, assuring himself that it is there. It is brown in colour. It appears small, but it is also far away. It is not possible to make out any features on it. Although he has not noticed it before now, he has the sense that its presence has been hovering at the edge of his mind, like a secret he was keeping from himself. Instantly, he knows his duty. He knows what he has to do.

8.

He does not remember the exact moment that he loses consciousness. Is it possible to remember such a moment? It is the cold more than anything that does it. Once he was in the water the island had disappeared from view and, at times, he doubted what he had seen with his own eyes. He had tried to swim east towards where he had seen the sun rise that morning, but as the day went on he had become disorientated. He only comes to as his head scrapes against the pebbles of the beach.

The island is much the same – a little smaller perhaps, the land a little flatter, though he is not certain. He estimates the centre and then plants the flag in the earth. It is torn at one side, but he will patch it. He would like to give the island a name, for the sake of future records, but because he does not know about the existence of Islands 1 to 20 and 22 and above, he feels he cannot. For the sake of clarity in his own mind, for the sake of naming it something, he names it Island 21.

His gun has survived the journey without damage. He takes it apart and cleans it. He takes his time and is thorough. Once it is reassembled he walks around the island, marking rocks at hundred-yard intervals with a cross of boot polish. Then he begins his run.

Acknowledgements

The Lee and de Zoysa families, Brendan Barrington, Alistair Daniel, Maura Dooley, Ben Felsenburg, James Gurbutt, Jenny Hewson, Courttia Newland, Nii Parkes, Rowan Routh and Peter Straus.

I would also like to acknowledge the generous assistance of Arts Council England.